ACCOMMODATIONS

Wioletta Greg

Translated from the Polish by
Jennifer Croft

TRANSIT
BOOKS

Published by Transit Books
2301 Telegraph Avenue, Oakland, California 94612
www.transitbooks.org

PUBLISHER & MARKETING CONTACT
Adam & Ashley Levy | editors@transitbooks.org

Originally published in Polish as Stancje by W.A.B. in 2017

LIBRARY OF CONGRESS CATALOGING INFORMATION AVAILABLE UPON REQUEST

DESIGN & TYPESETTING
Justin Carder

DISTRIBUTED BY
Consortium Book Sales & Distribution
(800) 283-3572 | cbsd.com

Printed in the United States of America

9 8 7 6 5 4 3 2 1

ACCOMMODATIONS

PRAISE FOR *SWALLOWING MERCURY*

"Achieves a form of literary alchemy that mesmerizes."

—*The New York Times*

"Warm, subversively funny and elegiac for a lost rural life but unflinching in its depiction of the darker strands of Polish society, *Swallowing Mercury* is constructed around a spine of resistance and individuality."

—*Times Literary Supplement*

"The book's appearance in the U.S. is a great gift . . . Greg's masterful first novel is charming, seductive, and sinister by turns."

—*Kirkus Reviews (Starred Review)*

"Greg's fictional debut combines the opposing literary styles of socialist realism and magic realism in intoxicating sentences that convey sensuous detail so delightfully that one feels as though one is eating watermelon outdoors in summer."

—*Booklist (Starred Review)*

"Marciniak's deft translation amplifies the engrossing sensory details of Greg's heartbreaking and enlivening novel."—*Publishers Weekly*

"This enchantingly elliptical fiction debut by British-domiciled Polish poet Wioletta Greg sparkles with a gem-like quality. Thanks to Eliza Marciniak's crisp translation, it brings freshness even to the crowded genre of the novella-sized bildungsroman, and can be devoured alongside the best coming-of-age translations of recent years, such as *Down the Rabbit Hole* by Juan Pablo Villalobos, *Signs Preceding the End of the World* by Yuri Herrera and *The Dead Lake* by Hamid Ismailov."

—*The Guardian*

"Wioletta Greg's first novel shines with a surreal and unsettling vigor. As an award-winning poet, Greg writes with a lyricism that brings alive the charms and dangers of Wiola's life."

—*The Financial Times*

"*Swallowing Mercury* is both magical and sinister, a memoir and a fairytale and, like Wiola, completely captivating."

—*The Irish News*

"Greg writes with a precise, strange charm, and the poet's acute sensitivity to detail. Little by little, I felt the presence of young Wiola appear beside me—vital, quick-witted and curious, picking her way through the dark woods of faith, family, sex, and politics as if in some melancholy fairytale. I experienced the book like a series of cool, clear drinks, each more intoxicating than the last."

—Sarah Perry, *author of The Essex Serpent*

"I have been utterly 'swallowed' by this odd yet oddly familiar folk novella—somewhere between memoir and fairytale—which has magic and menace in perfect measure."

—Sarah Baume, author of *Spill Simmer Falter Wither*

"I really loved this strange book, which is sometimes sinister and sometimes lovely, and many other things besides."

—Evie Wyld, author of *All the Birds, Singing*

"This book comes the way memory does, in fragments, like something overheard or glimpsed through a gap in a door. It might feel as if you shouldn't be listening, should turn away, but it is impossible to do so."

—Daisy Johnson, author of *Fen*

"A sparkling little gem of a book—there is a freshness and truthfulness in Wioletta Greg's writing that reminded me of Elena Ferrante and Tove Jansson."

—Carys Davies, author of *The Redemption of Galen Pike*

"*Swallowing Mercury* shows how the overwhelming forces of beauty, politics, mortality, violence, and hope can animate even the smallest moments of life."

—Rowan Hisayo Buchanan, author of *Harmless Like You*

I was trying to subdue the city by turning it into a projection of my own growing pains.

ANGELA CARTER, "Flesh and the Mirror"

1.
Vega Speaking

I'M HEADING TO THE VEGA HOUSE in Częstochowa at a quarter before sunset. It is Friday, September 30, 1994.

Rain streaks across the bus' windows. The dusk toys with the faces of the passengers and makes them into shapeless gray amoebas. When the driver turns the lights off, the crowd blurs together, looks like an expiring cetacean. Its bulky body heaves and swells and bursts into bundles of chives, dill, parsley poking out of people's plastic bags. I am nauseated by the odor of musty rugged jackets, wool, the tonics with which the women spritz their hair. Sitting on my suitcase I stare out the window, where the sunlight disappears into the poplars like when water closes over a cuttlefish.

Suddenly I think I see, standing up near the front of the bus, my old acquaintance Kamil, with whom I fell in love over the summer and then lost contact. That has to be him, I think, thrilled, squeezing myself and my suitcase towards him.

"Is it really you?" I ask, excited, grasping his leather jacket.

"Course it's me, honeycakes," responds this stranger as he eyes me up and down.

Humiliated, I try to withdraw, but the bus tilts over the ruts in the road and instead of taking a step backwards, I wind up with my cheek pressed against his hulking chest. The man, who is barely keeping himself upright, because he's drunk, squints his left eye, reaches out for my breasts, waving his hand around in the air for a while as though he were trying to pull back an invisible curtain and then starts feeling up the front pocket of my backpack, where a beef-stuffed roll has been festering since morning.

"Keep your hands to yourself, you filthy pervert!" shouts one woman who has witnessed the whole scene. At the word "pervert" the crowd disperses. The bus stops in the city's outskirts, and I get off like a fish leaping free from an aquarium; clinging on to the shelter at the stop I greedily suck down gulp after gulp of fresh air.

In my plaid duffel coat, auburn sweater and cords that are too long for me, I pull my suitcase down the side of the road, trying to avoid the puddles the pearly moon clasps and links this evening. A fog rises over the fields and instantly rids them of their stench of burning. Off in the distance looms a mushroom-like brick water tower. I pass a lumber yard, big factories and a warehouse of artificial Christmas trees where faded graffiti vie along the wall for attention: "Soviet Army=with you from birth" and "Widzew rules." From the direction of the city's center comes, wobbling along on the ruts, a dumper loaded up with scrap metal, and it splatters me with mud. Past the yellowed plane trees I glimpse two tall provisional buildings fronted with corrugated sheet metal. Over the first, attached by a wire to a rod, hangs a big sign scrawled in thick black Gothic script: "Waterproofing Exteriors Foundations Insulation"; over the second I can just make out the pink neon of the Vega workers' housing. I turn and go towards it.

I'm greeted at the door by a Dachshund, who sniffs over my sullied sneakers and wags her tail.

"That's Adelka. Our resident canine," says Natka Roszenko; she looks even prettier than she used to. Tanned, with her golden-brown hair cascading over her shoulders, she looks as though cut out of a fashion mag.

"I was a little worried you wouldn't find us. But why so frightened? As though you'd seen a ghost!"

I shrug.

"All well out in the country, with your folks?"

"Yes. Thanks."

"You can leave your things in the guardroom," she says and points out a makeshift booth of white plywood. "Waldek!"

In the little window, like in a puppet theater, the bald head of the property manager pops into and immediately out of view.

Then it's dark inside the Vega, and the manager gets up and squeaks over to the light switch in his Kubota slides. The neon flickers, and bright light floods the hallway, makes the glass bricks glow, sinks into the paneling, the crooked slats, the holes in the walls stopped up with newspapers.

Blinded, I follow the clack of Natka's heels. We enter a small area that looks like the storeroom of a textile merchant—on the wall unit, the desk and the floor lie jacquard blouses in plastic wrap, collapsed jute purses, lightweight scarves in garish colors, alpine slippers, linen tablecloths and Russian candy. Natka makes her way through this spoil tip of miscellany and, exhaling, she pushes aside a pair of pantyhose-clad mannequin legs as she sits at the desk. I sit in the chair facing hers, and in my panic I clutch the foot of one of these plastic legs in its adhesive mesh stocking.

"Tea?"

"I'd love some tea."

Natka leaps up, cracks the door, shrieks, "Waldek, give me back the water zapper!" Then she picks up a plastic container and taps a little bit of instant raspberry tea powder into a glass. In that dark Arcoroc, that powder looks more like rat poison.

"Maybe I should just quickly show you the room first, get it out of the way."

So we walk to the other end of the hallway, where between the bathroom and the rec room there's a little bedroom that is more like a cell, with mold stains on the walls, a wooden table covered with an oilcloth, a chair, a dilapidated daybed, aloe on the sill, an Eltra Hania boom box, a Gierek-era wardrobe, a sink slivered up by rust, and over it, a dry husk of a fern.

"To your liking then?" she asks in a tone that suggests

she has deduced that after dragging myself and my suitcase clear to the ends of the earth—or at least the city—I might be uninclined to return to the train station now, at night. "If so I'll take the money up front."

"Do you think I could get a little family and friends discount?" I ask, copying my mom's slick techniques, surprising even myself.

Smiling, Natka gets comfortable, crossing her legs, lighting a cigarette in a glass holder, disappearing into rising, coiling ribbons of smoke.

"Last year there was a college girl staying with us. She colleged for around two weeks, romped around the discos, and then after the first test she failed she up and got packing, and you can be sure she left none of what she owed behind," she says, keeping her poker face perfect, flicking her ashes into a vase. Then she regains her full range of expression: "And yet there I'd been that whole time, like some nincompoop, taking her fresh soup to preserve her from that super-nausea bowl they have the students eat at, where they say they sprinkle baking soda over everything."

I reach into my bag, resigned. This is before the zloty devaluation, so the stack of bills I hand her looks like a lot. But Natka throws it into her own bag without counting, and as the clock with the cross-eyed Mickey Mouse on it hits eight, she looks at herself in the little doors of the high-gloss wall unit, runs her hands through her hair and runs a tube of lipstick over her voluptuous pout.

"You'll have to excuse me, Wiola. I'm expected elsewhere. We'll see one another tomorrow."

"But . . ."

"Never you mind. Waldek's on duty, he'll show you everything you need to know. Oh, and make sure you remember your first dream in your new accommodations tonight—it might come true."

And she pops a red hooded cloak over her shoulders, and she walks out the door.

THE DREAM MENTIONED BY NATKA ROSZENKO puts me back at the train station in Częstochowa, where we pull up towards noon. I slide open the door to my compartment to step out with the mass of other travelers onto the platform and go through the passageway to get to the square from the other side, on Freedom Ave. It's overcast, although it was supposed to be sunny. The wind isn't much. By the shooting gallery the smells of dust and exhaust are overwhelmed by the stench of shit that wafts over from the pig farm nearby. Piglets' muzzles press against the fence like rubber ducklings. On the little square, called Kwadraty by the locals, brimstone devils go off, little mechanical dogs spread out on a blanket writhe until they stop and some old guy sings Christmas carols and hands out religious pictures. Fascinated by this city that brims over with village, I buy some soft-serve ice cream that comes out of a machine, look through a few rows of sunglasses hanging on display on wire racks.

A little while later I'm getting off of a tram and going inside a four-story concrete monolith on Home Army Ave, where down corridors that smell damp and like old paper and cigarettes pale students meander. At the registrar's office I collect the little booklet where all my grades will be recorded, write down my class schedule and while I'm there also discover that my name is not anywhere on the list of people granted university housing.

"It sure isn't," says the secretary. "Ain't nothing we can do about that, honey. You come from too close to Częstochowa, and we've got too little room in the dorms." She gobbles down two Ptasie Mleczkos at once and licks the chocolate rim around her mouth that expands the border around her mustache. "But you can rent your own accommodations, can't you?"

I don't respond because in the presence of the students standing behind me in line I don't really feel like explaining that after my grandmother's death I can't afford to rent a room.

I'm relieved to get out of the registrar's, and scraping alongside the tram tracks towards the city's center with the wheels of my suitcase, wobbly, I try to think where I could possibly spend the night. Obviously I could still catch a train to Myszków, and from there go by bus to my village, but . . . For starters, by buying a ticket back I'd be costing my mom extra, and secondly, I'm afraid to go back to Hektary, where for the foreseeable future I might wind up stuck.

At the intersection a tall boy with blond hair catches up with me. He's wearing a jean jacket with patches sewn on. He looks familiar. Against his tanned face his blue-gray eyes gleam like polished zlotys.

"Hey, where do you think you're headed with that suitcase?"

"Headed ahead."

"Do you recognize me?"

"Excuse me?"

"Never mind. Name's Piotrek." He offers me a sweaty palm.

"Wiola."

"Sorry to bug you on the street like this, I was just wanting to talk with somebody in the same year."

"We're going to be in the same year?"

"Sure looks like it. My mother talked me into trying to get in here, and as per usual she was right. If I hadn't listened to her after I took the exams I'd be scrubbing toilets with a toothbrush right now. Want to stop in for some coffee?" He nods towards a blocky two-storied building at the corner of Home Army and John Paul II.

At the coffee shop we sip prune liqueur that looks like tea and fight about books. I like *Lord of the Flies*; he prefers *Lord of the Rings*. I'm a *Tempest* girl; he's a *Catcher in the Rye* kind of guy. When the conversation turns to favorite movies, I squirm in my chair and smear Wuzetka filing up and down the laminated tabletop.

I can't tell him I actually don't even know any movies, I grew up in the fields, I spent half my childhood with the animals in the cowshed, in the attic and the pigsty, that I haven't seen TV in years because our old Rubin has long since been consigned to rest and recuperation in the dining room on the sunken floor next to the wall unit, while the film showings the mayor organized in the firehouse were finished the same day they started since someone stole all of the videocassettes, for some reason leaving only *Total Recall*, which after a few weeks everyone in the village knew by heart, but it really stuck with my good friend Older Lajboś, meaning he sniffed some neoprene adhesive and turned into an agent from Mars and ran all over the post-State Agricultural Farm fields disarming the straw coverings over the bushes. Last time I was in a movie theater was several years ago to see some Soviet movie about the war by Nikita Mikhalkov, I forgot the title because I was sidetracked by the fact that the viewers at the district culture house booed the performance of my school choir for its rendition of "Now We Can Move on from Lenin, Where Every Song's a Battle Cry."

We leave the coffee shop. The big Energetyka clock flashes four. Piotrek and I part ways in front of the Freedom Cinema, and I go back to trying to figure out what to do and where to stay since I know no one here and have no intention of giving up at this point, meaning calling my mom to say I didn't get into the dorms and that I'm not going to go to college after all and that I'll be home tonight and starting Monday I'll take that secretarial job she got me, and then I remember that for several years now on the outskirts of town an old acquaintance of ours from a neighboring village has been running a workers' residence. I race to the phone booth that is rusting away before the Megamart. I insert the necessary tokens and dial, hands shaking.

"Vega speaking," says the voice of Natka Roszenko.

"DING-DONG, TIME TO WAKE UP. No sleeping in class."
When I hear the theatrical whisper of Professor Brankowski, I jerk to in my chair as the other students in the room
all burst out laughing. It is their guffaws that rouse me
fully. Torn from my doze, I glance up at the blackboard,
which has Cyrillic scrawled all over it, and I remember
it's Monday already, and that I'm sitting in the rector's
building in a class on historical grammar.

"I'm sorry, Professor, but the Russians . . ."

"What Russians?" he interrupts. "Might we perchance
have seen them in our dreams?"

I return his gaze in terror. So that I don't have to
give any further explanation I just nod, although I could
swear that from Sunday night into early Monday morning as I lay shivering under the blanket in my unheated
room at the Vega I heard Russian voices, songs, shrieks,
which had persisted until dawn, preventing me from
sleeping. Professor Brankowski squints his rat eyes, does
a little loop in the front of the classroom, then strips off

his tweed jacket, hops up onto the bench in the first row, where I'm sitting, and presents to us a lotus pose we recognize from yoga. The girls are silent. The boys applaud.

I hurry out of the room, trying to get out of the rector's building before I run into anybody I know from my year, since I'm pretty sure they're planning to have, for the third night in a row, a meet-and-greet at Filutek, the students' bar.

It's past one, and since all I had for breakfast was a tiny cheese sandwich, I start to feel weak. I sit down on the bench next to the coatroom and close my eyes. The rumble of conversation that fills the hallways of the university takes a soporific effect on me. After spending eighteen years in the country, where a few passersby in the daytime on the rocky road might well be considered a crowd, this kind of human density reminds me of the processions when the fields were blessed, or for Corpus Christi, or for funerals, when they would make their way down the muddy trails like black caterpillars in clouds of limestone dust.

"Aren't you coming with us to Filutek?" Piotrek pipes up. Since the day we ran into each other at the registrar's, he's barely left my side for a second, carrying my backpack for me and sitting next to me in class.

"I have to get back a little earlier today."

"Where?"

"To the place I'm staying," I say, trying to get out of it because I have no desire to participate in these group outings. First of all, I don't have any money, and secondly, I feel uncomfortable in the company of my peers. I have less knowledge of the latest hits on MTV than I do of the collected works of Shakespeare, or Polish classics, or French, or above all Russian literature, which after the fall of the Polish People's Republic my father would bring home by the kilo from the pulping section of the Myszków paper mill where he worked. And when it comes to sex, as a teenager raised in the countryside I know quite a bit of theory, meaning more or less whatever I could glean from Michalina Wisłocka's *Practical Guide to Marital Bliss*, *Tropic of Cancer* by Henry Miller and *Memoirs of Fanny Hill*, plus the information drawn from my uncles' stories after they'd had a few too many drinks. In practice, all I've got is fifteen rushed lessons given to me by Natka Roszenko along with whatever I've been able to surmise from the men I've happened to cross paths with, among them the forty-year-old dance teacher I met over winter vacation two years ago and for whom I would walk five kilometers through snow drifts every day in order to reach the district's cultural center.

Stasikowa, the dressmaker, used to sew my clothes for me, but since her death I have at last been able to dress as I please, meaning contrary to fleeting fashion and to my mother, meaning I can be avant-garde. I bleach streaks of my hair and weave feathers and strands of leather into it, wear jasper amulets, wooden pendants, amber beads; I favor earthy tones: bronzes, dirty violets, copper, rotten green; natural materials: cotton, corduroy, linen; light-weight crocheted cardigans, wool sweaters, long skirts, bells, floral vests. Since coming to Częstochowa I've enjoyed wandering around town on my own, browsing used book stores, stores with Indian imports and places that sell used clothes by the kilo, where I read the labels on old garments; I smell the paints in art supply stores; in a notebook with a daffodil on it from the Wrocław Paper Mill, I write short stories about Marie Skłodowska-Curie, after whom my middle school was named, about the folk painter Séraphine Louis, about Sadako Sasaki of Hiroshima, who died of radiation poisoning, and not least I just sit out in the reading room in the hopes that I might run into Kamil somewhere.

"That's cool . . . Suit yourself," mutters an offended Piotrek, whose shadow falls upon a poster for a newly founded University of the Third Age. "I guess you're avoiding us."

He sits down next to me and hands me a Prince Polo bar.

We go to the Dwernicki Market, where from the various stalls we learn, in just a few minutes, all the most important national and international news, like that the cholera epidemic in Ukraine is spreading, after already affecting more than three hundred people, or about the disaster with the Estonian ferry that set sail for Sweden from Tallinn on Wednesday and wound up at the bottom of the Baltic, with eight hundred and fifty passengers, just after midnight, or about the image of Jesus appearing on a soybean-oil storage tank towering over a town in Ohio, or about the mutant mushrooms from the forests of Olesno, which you apparently can't buy due to the fact that, tainted by cesium following the Chernobyl disaster, they glow, or, finally, about hikes in the prices of bread, dairy products and coffee.

"Just think," says a florist to a man from a vegetable stand, who in his rumpled maroon windbreaker looks like a walking Krakowska kielbasa. "Last week butter cost sixteen thousand zlotys. Three days later, nineteen. I hate to think what's next!"

"That's nothing, my dear. Third of October alcohol goes up by fifteen percent. That'll mean your standard-issue vodka'll run around eighty-five thousand zlotys."

"You've got to be kidding me. I mean, it is what it is, but our liquor, too?" Having depressed herself, the florist returns to twisting maple leaves into roses. With the last of the money my mom gave me out of my grandpa's pension I purchase two loaves of wholegrain bread with pumpkin seeds, a mushroom-flavored spreadable cheese, tomato and some trail mix. At the same stall, alongside the zucchini and pumpkin and chrysanthemums, I see a dark green plant with little yellow splotches that looks, under the autumnal drizzle, like a severed alligator's tail.

"That's a bottle gourd," says the sausage. "I'll throw that in there for free. I've got to leave here in an hour or so, anyway, my bones'll be howling at me something awful."

"Oh, but—"

"I'll take it," says Piotrek. "My mom'll like it." And he stuffs the gourd into a plastic bag that says World Cup USA '94. Now it's like a crocodile hatchling, and we take turns carrying it down Holy Virgin Mary Ave, into a Żyrafa store to look at bags and as we amble back though the city center past Sienkiewicz High and all the way to Jasna Góra, where, according to local legend, there was once a huge underground dungeon.

"On Biegański Square, right where you stopped for a minute without even knowing it, there used to be this big pedestal with Vania on top of it," says Piotrek. "They used to call him the patron saint of shitting, just because there was this below-ground public restroom not too far from him."

"Who's Vania?"

"This soldier in this billowing half-shelter, with a PPSh-41 and an olive branch. I guess after '89 there was a big push to get rid of him, so by World Youth Day, when it was held here in '91, I guess it was gone. This friend of my mom's who was working in this parliament deputy's office had this guy who kept coming in, he'd been a pilot in the Battle of Britain, and he had this money-saving scheme to sever Vanka's half-shelter and just give it to Piłsudski. In the end, the marshal got a coat of his own, and all that remains of Vanka is this little ditty: "There once was a soldier atop a high column, facing the church, his ass to the Presidium.""

WALDEK CRACKS THE LITTLE DOOR of his manager's booth, covered over in a map of the night sky, and proudly presents me his solved Rubik's cube.

"Howdy, milady. Look, I got it in an hour this time."

I give him an admiring nod.

"That's really great," I say. "It'd take me all day to do it."

"Now, now. What's got our college gal so grumbly today?"

"The bus was packed."

"At this time of day it's always Sodom and Gomorrah. You must've noticed on your route, kid, how many different businesses they've opened up these days. There's the waste screening plant and the water bottling plant and the Christmas decorations depot. Who knows what else. Częstochowans have spread so it's gotten hard to keep up with them, but once you pass through that gate it's the same clusterquag as ever. At one time this here was the very edge of town. The bus would stop at Żyzna, and you had to walk another kilometer from the station to get to the factory. And there were only a couple of 'em: morning and afternoon. Although that's nothing, college kid. They say that underneath these barracks there was once this network of shelters they built during the Cold War, and they say one of them had—" He stomps his slipper on the floor.

"Waldek—" I interrupt, since I'm barely managing to avoid collapse. "Natka said something about soup for dinner?"

"Did she now?" He stands up with evident displeasure. "We'll get that right out for you, then. I'll just go and get that little heater-upper from her office."

He leaves with a fistful of keys and, limping, walks to the opposite end of the hall and into Natka's office. Once he's back he shows me two yellow packets of ramen noodle soup.

"Crab or golden chicken. Which does our college gal prefer?"

I figure I might as well pick the first, since I know they taste identical. I do and then sit on the stool and survey the area, where the main motifs are not, as it seemed to me at first, dangling cables, the remaining half of a mirror hanging over the sink, the brush, the shaving paste, the pack of Polsilver razors or the collection of empty beer cans, but rather, pinned to the thin straw liners on the walls, pennants of football clubs from the West and yellowed pages from an astronomy magazine.

Waldek rinses two mugs in the sink and sprinkles the contents of the bags into them; when the little pot begins to boil, he pours the water into them. As the coils of the noodles swell, and the small space fills with the scent of soy sauce, he serves our dinner on the metal lid from a box of chocolates.

"Spicy, eh?"

"Hot as heck."

"It'll burn off all our sins."

"So what's that?" I ask hesitantly, pointing to the rose he has tattooed on his left hand.

Waldek is silent but for slurping down his soup. He wipes his mouth with the sleeve of his patterned sweater.

"Oh, what's the point, college kid." He waves his hand. "It's ancient history. I was a troublemaker in my youth—no surprise, of course, considering I was raised without a mother, out past Częstochowa. I finally ran out of room to maneuver and ended up getting arrested. They put me upriver at first and then back here at the Herby Jail, but when they let me out I got a gig at a factory, which is how I became a Częstochowan. At first I was living in the Bermuda Triangle, where I got my dental work done pretty quick. Well, you know, I tended to talk back as a kid, so of course they went straight for the kisser and knocked out all my teeth."

"Bermuda Triangle?" I say.

"It's in the slums, between Mała, Mokra and Stawowa. Under communism they got the whole seedy underbelly set up there so's they could keep their eye on it. While I was living on Krakowska Street I'd hardly ever show my face on Mała Street. But this once when I was still wet behind the ears my aunt and uncle sent me to the blind pig to pick up some of the strong stuff. And I go on down to this basement where I think a Mr. Bobas resides, and instead I find this dirt floor, you get me, the chick with no clothes on lying on a pile of rags, not moving. I think to myself I better fuck off quick, I don't want any problems, but this chick somehow resurrects from the dead and jumps me with a whisk and chases me down the street butt naked!"

"And you like astronomy?" I change the subject even as I choke on my own laughter.

"Oh, you know. Got bored in the slammer, started picking up this and that to read. Around three years ago I secured myself this whole huge stack of *Urania* issues at this used bookstore on Copernicus." His eyes sparkle, and he wriggles a little on his hard stool, probably because of the Antabuse implant he has in his rump. "I brought 'em in here to my booth so I could do a little reading, time to time." He unpins from the straw liner a page with scribbles in the margins. "Get a load of this, Miss College Kid." He puts on his glasses and opens an issue from the second of October, 1938. "'In the first four months we have observed five comets,'" he reads. "'We'll see what the next months bring.'" He gives me a significant glance, but I don't immediately get what he's saying. "Five comets *and* meteor showers right before the outbreak of World War II? You don't see where I'm heading here?"

"Yes! I think so."

"The guy that wrote that, this guy Antoni Czubryński, he was an astralist and a Polish freemason, and his wife had a perfect mastery over occultism, palmistry, graphology, Kabbalah, Asian beliefs, you name it. Their daughter could see the future. That was her professional occupation, actually."

Amazed by all his knowledge, I give him another admiring nod.

"Five comets in just the first half of the year!"

"And meteor showers!"

"Look here, kid." With a trembling hand, he pulls out a crumbling page from 1920. "Back then they didn't even know of Pluto yet, you know, they wouldn't discover it for another ten years, and yet here they are talking about some planet on out past Neptune. Some pretty sharp SOBs, wouldn't you say? This here is a thing about the canals on Mars."

But now my mug falls out of my hands, and the rest of my cold soup splashes over my cords, which I just got through washing in the sink. I don't think about that, though. I look from the engraving of Orkisz's Comet that makes it look more like a roundworm to Waldek's face, sweaty from the hot soup, which has suddenly, unexpectedly reminded me of that of my dead father. My dad was a taxidermist, beekeeper and angler. Looking through nature books, he'd spend hours on end telling me tales of rare species of fish and birds, and then with great relish he would catch them, then kill them.

LYING ON THE DIVAN with the dachshund and snacking on poppy-seed pretzel sticks, I gaze out at the October sky.

"Is that pretty?" I say to Adelka, who seems to understand because she jumps up onto the windowsill, gets over by the aloe plant and lifts her little black nose. Someone must have scattered glitter out there, or taken a cosmic pick to the bottom of things and let out clouds of fireflies from that black hole—and for a second I feel like the dung beetle, whose vision is so frail it hardly sees a thing in its vicinity, and yet its every movement is in keeping with the light of the Milky Way.

From *Urania* I learn that the constellations we see in the sky may no longer be in existence, separated from us by a billion light years, and that astralism has nothing to do with horoscopes, but is instead the study of cults of celestial bodies in ancient myths. Next I read the old Hutsul legend of Saint George, who sits on the moon taming wolves with his violin song, and after that I read about teleportation by means of infrared radiation, about Martian channels that crisscross in recurring patterns as though the products of intelligent design, about the framework of the Milky Way and the nebulae according to Lindblad's theory:

Let us imagine the inhabitant of an island covered in dense forest. The inhabitant is unable, for various reasons, to leave his territory, nor is he able to move freely within its bounds. Needless to say, an unfortunate soul such as this one will be unable to know what his island looks like. As it turns out, we find ourselves in a similar situation on this island-world of ours—in other words, our galaxy—to which we are condemned, without the possibility of free movement, with our view of what is further afield, and in particular that of the immediate environs of our galaxy, obscured by clouds of opaque matter.

"Clouds of opaque matter," I read over, now aloud, gazing into the ceiling, where two fat flies—among fall's few survivors—trace figure eights. The engraving of the Milky Way makes me think of the shells of the snails that would dash madly from the calcareous soils of my village in the Polish Jurassic Highland, the place where I was born and raised.

I set *Urania* down on the linoleum next to a sleeping Adelka, thinking how the hundred-year-old black-and-white photographs of nebulae in the Orion constellation would no doubt be of interest to the man with whom I lost touch in August, the man I miss so much these days.

Kamil, a graduate student in ethnography, would come in his Fiat from Częstochowa to Hektary to record folk songs and tales since the spring of last year. One June afternoon he came up to me in the courtyard and asked me if I might be able to show him to a couple of places where he'd be able to take some photographs. I splashed my face with water from the hose, tamped down my rowdy hair, and—to the total outrage of my mom and grandma and the neighbor lady—led him, little by little, down a trail through the mown fields past the juniper shrubs, where once there flowed a river, and stemless carline thistles bloomed.

That meadow by the limestone mines in chaos smelled so strongly of wildflowers that I got dizzy. Not heeding the admonitions of my mother, who always insisted I behave "as a lady must" when in company, I lay down in an empty reinforced concrete gutter—abandoned by builders in the eighties—on the balk between State Agricultural Farm fields and took a look up at the sky through the inside of a snail's shell.

Kamil sat down near me, on marlstone, snapped some pictures, softly singing a folk tune I didn't recognize about a girl who grazed on a peacock's meadow.

AFTER WATCHING THE NIGHTLY cartoons in the common room, I return to my own room, and tripping over my suitcase yet again, I decide to unpack: with a disposable handkerchief I wipe off the table, the windowsill and the shelves in the cabinet, where in a few minutes I have laid out underwear, pantyhose, a toiletry bag with Bambino ointment, a toothbrush, toothpaste, a tube of mascara, what little is left in my Constance Carroll compact and sanitary pads. In the vase, I replace the dusty plastic roses with a bunch of heather from a ditch on my way back to the Vega, and—feeling pleased—I lie back down on the divan. The first time in my life I've ever had my own room, and it's in a place named after the brightest star, I think, and as a sudden influx of happiness starts to soothe me to sleep, the hallway thumps with the hit pop song I recognize from senior prom and weddings: *Wheel of Fortune*, by Ace of Base. "*What you gonna tell your dad? It's like a wheel of fortune.*" I jump to my feet and peer out from my room. "*What you gonna tell your dad if this wheel lets you down?*"

From the common room a man in a messy plaid shirt runs out; then he dashes up the stairs. A second man, similar to the first, staggers in his wake, his eye black, in a bluish-lilac tracksuit made of thin, almost transparent polyester.

"*Sergey! Sergey! Zhdi menya!*" this second figure bellows. "*Ya nye khotyel!*" Clinging to the railing, he tries to climb the stairs, but he staggers and falls several steps down, onto the muddied mat. And as if this weren't enough, now a woman peers out from the common room, her hair an angry blonde, paper curlers on her head, her body wrapped in a bathrobe made of velour.

"*Alex? Vy zhivyotye?*" she asks and nudges the man lying on the floor with an embroidered slipper.

The man called Alex sits up on the floor now and hiccups. The woman giggles, waves her hand and returns to the common room, whence shreds of the Ace of Base song can still be heard, interwoven with lines of dialogue from a Russian film. I'm thinking about retreating into my room when suddenly from upstairs there begin to fall the guts of some pillows, duvets without covers, white like salami's moly coating, clothes and moccasins.

"*Poshol von. Ya nye khochu zhyt' s toboy v odnoy komnatye!*" shrieks Sergey.

Alex meekly collects his scattered things, clambers up to the top of the stairs, turns when he gets to the second floor and disappears down the dark hallway.

"Waldek!" I knock on his booth and peek in at our manager, who with a blissful expression is peeling an apple with a penknife.

"What is it, college kid," he replies so calmly it's almost as though he is completely unaware of the scene playing out in the hallways of the Vega.

"You think you could call?"

"Call who?"

"The police?"

"The People's Republic of China, why don't I."

"But they'll kill each other."

"Well what am I supposed to—" He waves his hand. "Don't worry, university gal. The twins always horse around a little when they get back from the market by the Promenade. They chase after one another, get tired, drink whatever they've got left to drink, and then they hit the hay."

"But who are these people?"

"They're Russians, Russians who work the markets. Sergey and his twin brother Alex. They're good kids."

"And the woman in the curlers?"

"That's Ludmila, a distant relation of our beloved Natka. She got here not too long ago and works over at the pavilion of what used to be the Adria, but don't ask me what she does there, exactly, because I have no idea."

"Where's the Adria?"

"The Adria is, or was, on Home Army Avenue, where you take your bus to school. When I first joined up with the Częstochowans, that was the best place to go dancing in the whole town. Every Sunday from ten on they would serve beer out on the patio. They'd only sell it to you as part of a combo that also included an appetizer. The appetizer consisted of a piece of cheese with butter on it and sprinkled with spicy paprika. Now, you would collect this appetizer in this one place, but you couldn't eat it, because over yonder the lady had to see it in the client's hand in order to sell him a beer. So you had all these guys standing around in line, nice and polite like, with their appetizer out. You could get two bottles of beer for every appetizer. One day I stop by after I get off, take a look, and what do I see on stage? Not the stripper that's supposed to be there, that's for sure. Instead there's some half-naked jackass that's walloping around, getting groovy. I'm about to head out since that ain't really my thing, but then I look a little closer, and can't believe my eyes. It's my old pal Gray Jurek, in the flesh, the same guy who always tooted his own horn, saying he was some kind of sex demon. I don't know whether he was just tired that night, or if he'd had too much liquid courage, but he goes and gets all tangled up in his own underpants and just falls flat, right beside this table where some bigwig is having his leg meat jelly. And everybody's dying. The head of the Adria vanishes into the back. And this red spider sets his fork down, gets up from his chair, puts his hands on his hips and says: 'Rocco, sir! Rocco, sir, please!'"

I return to my room. I hang my now somewhat sweaty clothing on the chair and try washing up in my sink, splashing water all over the linoleum just because I'm not brave enough to go out into the hallway to the open bathroom. I change into my flannel pajamas and snack on trail mix, staying up till midnight writing a letter to my mother.

When the Vega quiets down, meaning that all that can be heard from the common room are the low murmurs of the television, I turn onto my stomach, press the edge of my blanket into my crotch, and moving rhythmically, I picture myself as Rocco, standing naked on a stage. All around me tiny specks of dust, lit by little overhead lamps like spotlights, spiral and dance, crashing together and flying apart until at last they collapse onto their dark audience.

I WAKE UP, FROZEN, AT AROUND TEN, and once I've put my feet on the hot water bottle Natka insists is a suitable replacement for heating in my room, I turn on the Eltra Hania. After reporting on the mail bombs in America, they play the song *Last Christmas* by George Michael. I push the duvet aside and wrap the throw around me and look out the window. It is December, and midmorning is cool and smells of soot and benzene. I leave my room in search of Waldek, to ask him for some hot water so I can make tea. His booth is empty. In his chair dozes Adelka, curled up and whimpering as though wrestling with something in her dreams. I head for the common room, parting the beaded curtains and standing on the threshold breathing in the fragrance of freshly brewed coffee, which stifles the disgusting stench of the previous evening's festivities.

I'm greeted by one of the Russian twins I saw running around the Vega. My eye chases after the sound of his "*Dobroye utro*," finding him in the corner. He is sitting in just his underwear, with his legs crossed. His foot moves from side to side in its slipper; his face wears the satisfied expression of a man in a five-star hotel somewhere in the Canary Islands, not someone living in an unheated workers' residence. Unaccustomed to the sight of a naked male stranger, I look away. But as I start to withdraw from the common room, he, to my surprise, starts to talk to me in Polish:

"I have noticed that you people from Częstochowa have a crow on your city's coat of arms." He points to the one pinned to the door frame.

"That's not all!" I smile. "The current mayor of Częstochowa's name is Wrona." The word must be similar in Russian, because he seems to understand it means crow.

"You are kidding."

"No, it's true."

"Well. I don't suppose you know why in some Russian towns the domes on the churches are all scratched up?"

"No, I don't."

"It's because the crows play this game where they take the lid off of a jar of mayonnaise, and they slide down off the roof on it, like little snowboarders."

"Seriously?"

"Or they slide down the church domes, and then at the last second, they just brake with their claws."

"You're kidding!"

"Or they toss nuts down onto the crosswalks. When it's don't walk, the cars are cracking nuts for them, and when it's time for the pedestrians to cross, that's when the crows swoop down and gobble up their little snack. I used to have a crow that lived with me once. Karkusha was her name. Kara, I called her."

"Was she a rescue?"

"These babies were too big, and they fell out of their nest, and of course there was no way to stuff them back in there again. They were big, but they couldn't fly yet, and of course they would get killed if we left them there in that park. So each of us—I remember it was three of us, me and my friends—we each took one of the baby crows home. At first I thought a crow like that was pretty stupid, that its brain was the same as a chicken or a pigeon. That's what I thought. It's only now I realize, and it's even scientifically proven, that the intellect of a crow or a raven or whatever is actually closer to that of a monkey or an ape. They're really very clever. And of course being in my home she taught me all about that, with her behavior, all the things she figured out how to do."

"Did she follow you around?"

"Yes. And she would beg for food! Later on I made her a nest, and she would drag anything she could find that was shiny into that nest. But the best was the time my mom had these sovkhoz cucumbers, and they had these little yellow flowers, religiyki."

"Reliwhat?" I try, but he ignores me.

"Every now and again you had to pluck some of their flowers off, so that there wouldn't be as many of them, but the ones there were would be bigger. And my mom would do that, she'd pluck them and put them in a little pile. And that crow was there, flying around, observing. The next day the neighbor comes and says, 'I'm going to kill this crow of yours!' she shrieks. 'What are you talking about? Why?' we ask her. 'I'm going to end up with no cucumbers because of her! She ripped off all the little flowers and left piles of them all over.'"

FOR SAINT NICHOLAS DAY we meet in the common room, eat the broth with noodles Natka brought in a plastic canister and play Russian Schnapsen. As he makes the game's first bid, Sergey hums: "*Pust' vsyegda budyet solntse.*" Waldek, humming along, says pass. I, although I have no idea why, bid one-twenty, fervently praying that Alex tops me, since with a king and queen of diamonds I have no shot at making that many points.

"Russian soups were thicker," Alex pronounces as we finish eating and set our dishes in the corner by the Christmas tree. "I'd add chicken, potatoes, macaroni, sautéed pepper, carrot."

"Bay leaves?" I ask.

"Leaves, chopped parsley," Alex continues, staring at the deck.

"Could you grow bay leaves in Siberia?"

"Over where we lived, over by Omsk? No, university woman, bay leaves grew in the Caucasus. But what I really loved was this soup that had meatballs in it. But also pelmeni, and manti, which are similar to pelmeni, but bigger and steamed, and chebureki, which are like potato pierogi except for three times the size, and you fry them on both sides in the pan, and then inside: meat in onion. We called fish soup ukha."

Waldek can take no more of Alex's culinary reminiscences and leaves the common room for a minute, returning with a can of sardines, which he opens with his penknife. He wipes off his greasy fingers on a flap of shirt sticking out from the bottom of his sweater.

"If you wish I'll tell you the story of my fiancée," he proclaims.

"Yeah!" we all cry in unison, and setting down our cards forget immediately who was bidding what as we fix our eager eyes on the manager of the Vega. Alarmed by our volume, Natka, who stayed later than usual today in order to finish up some paperwork, sticks her head into the common room.

At first Waldek says nothing, heightening our curiosity. Then he sits down by the heater, stretches out his legs and takes a crumpled photograph out of his wallet.

"Her name was Adelka." He shows us a petite blonde.

"Adelka?" I ask in surprise.

"Right you are, college gal. Our wiener dog's named after her."

"So where did you two meet?" asks Natka, who finds she can't hold out any longer and comes into the common room and sits in the armchair opposite Waldek.

"Church," Waldek responds.

"Church?!" I shriek, for the thought of a feverishly praying Vega manager Waldek seems as unlikely to me as the Martian canals described by prewar issues of *Urania*.

"It was in August, right around my uncle's funeral. There I am heading for Stradomka to cool my heels a little, just sit by the water like when I was a boy. Then I start to get hungry and head back into town. It's hot. The crowds keep tripping me up, and these pigeons, these kids, dogs, whatever all else, pilgrims waving pennants, hawking knockoff Black Madonnas. It's a madhouse, and I need out. So I escape into Saint Sigismund Church, just because it happens to be open. I amble down along the middle there. Silence. And the temperature is perfectly cool. I dip my fingers in that holy water, sit down, look around, kind of uncomfortable, but there right next to me is this girl, small or petite or whatever, and she's just bawling. Bawling! You can believe me or not, but even though I'm not one for romance or relationships, her I fell head over heels for at first sight. We went and got some ice cream, and then we went to the movies, and then we went for some vodka, and somehow it ended up a couple days later she was living with me in that rough neighborhood of mine. The days flew by, one after the other, and we saw nothing of the world besides each other. The lengths I would go to, all that hustle, for her to get her garb and her lipsticks, her leather boots, though I can assure you she never asked me for a thing. She was meek like you can't even imagine. She worked nights at a pasta factory. Every day she'd wash that orange apron of hers in the sink, iron it, and then she'd come back in the mornings with bags full of macaroni: shells, spirals, what have you, although we never ate them, we thought they were terrible, we just gave them to the neighbors.

"As you're surely aware, Częstochowa is small, and everyone knows everyone. One day after my shift I stopped by Sir. I wanted to get an engagement ring for Adelka and figuring that that was where the Gypsies and Romanians all sold their stolen gold. So I go in. And sitting at the counter there's this guy, Gutek, maybe you guys know him, head of the mafia in Częstochowa. Gutek must have had a lot to drink because he starts to blabber about this villa on Mirowska that this guy who had a mirror factory built over by the stud farm.

"'Zbych doesn't force his girls to do anything,' he says and glances over at Vadim, that Romanian who comes to Natka sometimes for duds, like he was wanting to accuse him of sending his women begging. Vadim gets real stiff, his hands go white around his beer bottle. The waiter runs off into the back, and we kind of slouch down a little because everybody knows all hell's about to break loose. You could tell Vadim kept on hesitating whether he wanted to beat the shit out of Gutek or not, but in the end he lets it go. Good thing, too—if he'd gotten into it he'd have been pushing up daisies in the Aniołowski Woods. 'Believe you me, one of his girls,' says Gutek, 'has been conning her man this whole time saying she's got the night shift at some pasta plant. Every day before she leaves she puts this little orange apron in her bag, heads to Tesco, buys the cheapest shells, spirals, rigatonis she can find and dumps them into different bags."

"I knew what they were saying off the bat. I ran out of there without a word. I wandered the town in desperation half the night. Adelka, for the love of God, Adelka!, I hollered. Why? When the shock passed I went home, and don't even ask me what I was planning on doing."

"Of course!" shrieks a fascinated Ludmila. The twins glance at Natka.

"And? Did you find her at home?" Natka asks, her voice trembling a little.

"Did I find her at home. Gutek caught on, had her sent for."

"And? Did you try to find her?" I ask.

"College kid, I've been looking for her ever since," he whispers, then repeats: "Ever since." His eyes glimmer, nearly water over.

AT SIX TWENTY P.M. MOSCOW TIME, Russian aircrafts attack Grozny. The bombs damage four power stations and a television tower.

The halls of the Vega are exceptionally quiet. Not even the TV in the common room is on. The potted palm curls up its leaves from the cold. Slowly the trail of muddy tracks that stretches from Natka's office to the front doors of the Vega—which wobble on their hinges like they serve in a saloon—dries. Everyone but Sergey—who keeps reading books in his room on the second floor, playing songs every so often on his harmonica, playing himself in chess, packaging his jute bags for market—is sitting around the space heater, their eyes never wandering from its orange spirals.

"When we were living in Siberia," Alex interrupts the silence, "there was this one cow named Apryelka."

"Apryelka . . ." I repeat, because it strikes me as a nice name.

"Because she was born in April," Alex explains. "That cow really made an impression on me. When she sensed we were about to sell her, she completely changed her behavior. She just wandered around mooing, with these tears pouring down her face like peas. Eventually my parents went to this struggling sovkhoz, where they bought Mayka. Mayka had been brought up under deep communism, getting her ears pierced, with this little number put in there. So then we went and took her home with us and started to just hang around a little where she was, started cleaning her, giving her different types of tasty treats, and it was like she could tell, I mean that we were really taking care of her, that we cared about her, and she became more similar to a dog or something. We never had to worry about her. We knew that if she went off somewhere she'd always come right back."

"How'd you land in Siberia?" Waldek asks.

"My dad was in the military, they transferred him there. Meanwhile my grandpa got his electrician's degree, and everybody told him not to enlist, because there had to be a man left in the village, but he wouldn't hear of it. I'm not going to just sit around with the girls, he said. Although I think he regretted it later. In Smolensk, or not Smolensk, further west, as they were pulling up in their train there was this German flying his plane over them so low you could see his ugly mug and see that he was smiling, but our boys couldn't do anything about it since all they had was just a couple of rifles. One day this guy Georgii comes up and says, Hey, you, look, there's some lard there hanging off of that bush. Well, let's eat it, hollers my grandpa, because they hadn't had anything to eat in two days or some such. He runs out and looks and what do you know, those smoked scraps were actually a piece of the nurse's ass from when she'd stepped on a mine as she was trying to run off."

"Where'd you learn to speak such great Polish?" I ask Alex.

"I learned it just like Natka did: from Poles."

"But Natka grew up here, in the countryside, in Poland."

"Alright, alright. I will confess. My mother taught me, her dad was a Pole; he lost his parents in Siberia when he was five, or maybe four, years old. All my pops could say in Polish was 'hello,' but whenever he got pissed off about something, he'd always swear in very old-fashioned Polish."

"Why doesn't Sergey speak Polish?"

"He does, he just doesn't like to. He's weird because when he was little he fell out of his stroller. First we were living in Georgia, in Tbilisi, because they'd sent our father there. Then we spent almost a year in Azerbaijan, in Baku and Nagorno-Karabakh, where there were riots."

"You saw them?"

"I didn't, because we were residing in a big apartment block by the army unit, but I saw the tanks heading in, and I'd wake up at night because of the shooting."

"Were you scared?"

"Me? Nah. I actually wanted to go out there, but my mother would not permit me. All of us wanted to be in the army. Our father bought us a Makarov pistol that was just like the real thing, just blue so you could tell the difference, and you'd load these little caps into it. Plus we had shishigi."

"What are shishigi?"

"GAZ-66 military four-by-fours. Sergey and I were always hanging around the unit. There was this hole in the fence somewhere. You weren't allowed to get into it, but we'd do it anyway, and one time I met Azer, this boy about my age. We started hanging around together, just hanging out and then whenever the unit alarm bell went off, we'd go up and hide in one of the army towers . . ."

Suddenly the beads at the entrance part, revealing Sergey's head. Having overhead his brother's story, he taps his forehead and recites something in Russian.

"What did he say?" I ask Alex, because although I supposedly studied Russian all through school I understand very little of it.

"It's a poem by Fyodor Tyutchev," answers Alex.

"What does it say?"

"Let's see . . . 'Russia can't be comprehended with the mind. Russia is unique. All you can do with Russia is believe.'"

Just then, as I'm about to mention the bombing of Grozny to the twins, Adelka leaps out of my lap and runs out into the hallway. The doors to the Vega open. At the clacking of Natka's heels, the brothers get up, turn around and race up the stairs.

"What are they running away from her for?" I ask Waldek. "Haven't they paid their rent?"

"What do you mean, college gal? You don't know?"

"I guess not."

"They're both in love with her."

"Well, what does she say about it?"

"Natka being Natka, she doesn't say a thing. She's still stuck on her old beau, Scurvy, who is alleged to have died in a car crash as he was making his way to Deutschland."

I DON'T GO HOME OVER THE CHRISTMAS HOLIDAY, much to my mother's disappointment, the official reason being I need to prepare for my Old Polish Literature exam, the unofficial reason being I just want to stay at the Vega, even though it's true it's just as cold as it is on my family's stone home on the pond, heated by a single coal-burning stove. Yet my accommodations in Częstochowa are more peaceful, and nobody turns out the lights at ten p.m. By the twenty-sixth, when snow has covered the Vega's drive, and the fruits of the plane trees look like coconuts on their bared branches, I begin hungrily lamenting my decision to spend the holidays here. I miss my mom, who would make the most of New Year's Eve and buy sangria and bake a glazed cocoa cake in her electric pan. We'd munch on delicacies left over from Christmas Eve: poppy seed cake, the crumbs of Christmas wafers, red borscht with dumplings, cabbage with beans.

I go out and pause by the stairs, where Sergey is playing his harmonica. Getting lost in its melody, I remember my father over the holidays in eighty-seven, dragging home— my mom and I had preferred not to know where he had found it—a nearly two-meter-tall spruce tree, which he subsequently decided to reduce in size. He brought a saw from the barn and sat down on the linoleum, now splattered with spruce needles, then spent the next twenty minutes pondering how best to trim this trophy. My mom, anticipating problems, immediately determined she would vacate the premises, heading to the neighbor lady's, while I stayed behind. To make my father's deliberations go a little quicker, I went to the kitchen to make him some tea, but when I returned, the spruce was still lying exactly where he'd first laid it down. My father was now cradling the saw, using some stalk to play this ballad on it by the folk group Kapela Czerniakowska: "Over the houses a gray fog, a cold wind that outspread it, and every day to the factory went the factory girl."

Sergey, having noticed me huddled up on the bench by the driveway, stops playing, sticks his harmonica in his pocket, comes up, wraps me in his big scarf and leads me through the back of the Vega to the one-story structure behind it, which Natka rents out to people for storage. He slides a key into the padlock. We enter the structure, which smells like grease and carbide and sawdust; between two posters of a busty *Baywatch* Pamela Anderson there hangs a square plywood target. Sergey opens a metal case that sits in the corner by a pile of damp cardboard boxes and presents me with a succession of daggers and knives.

It's cold. My breath glides down those polished blades. That steel reflects our faces: mine small and pale, his tanned from the markets. His jaw juts out like the Terminator's.

After examining the contents of the case, we stand in the center of the room. Sergey demonstrates a knife toss, landing a bullseye. I applaud him, then try to imitate his movements precisely, positioning the blade as he does, along my index finger, but every time I hurl the knife it bounces right off the plywood and lands on the sawdust-strewn ground. After a dozen failed attempts I've completely forgotten the storehouse chill. I press part of an icicle to the cut on my finger and force my rapidly weakening hands to keep trying to hit that target. Sergey sits straddling the metal case and watches me, laughing. Finally, bored, he stands behind me and arranges my shoulders, thighs and back so that I'm standing how I should be. Now, finally, the blade I launch tears into the white plywood and sticks deep in the heart of the target. I squeal with joy and throw my arms around Sergey's neck; Sergey blushes, takes me by the waist and lifts me up like I'm a straw doll. I spread my arms like I'm a hawk being released into the world by my father; I gulp down the cold air and dust. Coming back onto the concrete floor, facing away from Sergey, I accidentally brush against his stomach, then his thighs. I also feel his penis, hard against my bottom. Turned on, I turn around to face him. Sergey takes my hand and puts my bleeding finger into his mouth and sucks it for a moment; then he leans down and—his lips smelling of iron—kisses me with tongue and slowly, so that I don't trip over any of the knives we've thrown around, he moves me towards the corner of the room. Very aroused, I lean into the cool wall. Sergey unbuttons my jacket, kisses my nipples through my shirt, leaving patches of moisture on the cotton; whispering something in Russian, he lifts up my shirt and sticks his tongue into my navel.

"Having fun, my pets?"

Wearing her sheepskin coat and the suede boots that go up to her knees, Natka is sitting on the storeroom's threshold, smoking a cigarette. Only now do I catch the fragrance of the tobacco and her sweet perfume. I tug my shirt down, leap aside.

Natka stomps out her cigarette butt on the cement and comes up to Sergey, who's still standing by the wall, keeping his hands at his sides.

"What did I tell you?" says Natka in a menacing tone I've never heard her use before, and then, as hard as she can, she punches Sergey in the face.

AT A QUARTER BEFORE EIGHT I'm awakened by police sirens. The indigo lights come spilling through the shutters. Still half asleep, I sit up in the daybed and wonder whether by any chance the VCR in the common room might have jammed, making these just the effects of *Miami Vice.*

I rub my eyes and try to look outside, but scraps of wet snow cling to the panes, obscuring my view of the little square in front of the hotel.

Someone knocks softly at the door. I climb out of bed and turn the key. Ludmila slips into my room. Her swollen face, edged with yellow curlers, looks like a tansy bouquet. She takes a look around my room, opens the wardrobe and hands me a pair of jeans, a shirt and Natka's boots. Her grip is shaky. In a kind of frenzy she then throws all of my other things into my suitcase.

"Wait, what's going on, Ludmila?"

"Eet ees better if you do not know."

"Where's Natka? Did the brothers get into another fight over her?" I ask anxiously, zipping up the jeans.

"Eet ees better if you do not know."

I dress as fast as I used to for morning roll call at summer Scouts camp and in two minutes am ready to go.

"*Klas,*" chuckles Ludmila, though I can tell she is spooked. "*Idi, nie bojsia.*" She points to the wardrobe.

"You want me to hide in there?"

"*Nyet.*"

"Where do you want me to go, Ludmila?" I press, trying to make sense of her words.

In the hallway, footsteps rumble ever louder, Ludmila goes up to the wardrobe, opens it wide and in one fell swoop has ripped out its back. She points to the dark space this leaves, covered in cobweb fringe and slaps a note into my hand. I skim it: "Ludmila will give you a package. Put it under the floorboard by the exit to the shelter. We'll give you your suitcase. I love you. Natka."

"Be on," whispers Ludmila, putting back the back of the wardrobe before slamming the door to my room shut behind me.

As I turn around, I hear, coming from behind the door, Adelka whimpering, but I can't go back now, it's too late to say goodbye to her. I go down the stairs, holding on to the damp concrete wall. Darkness cozies up to me, supplying plush and cobwebs. "You can do this, you can do this," I tell myself over and over.

At last I reach a ruined room that looks more like a large cell. Rows of cables run along the walls. Every now and then my fingers catch on metal bands, nodules, valves, and the odor of mouse droppings and dust and the carcasses of mice catches in my nose. I swallow in an attempt to get rid of the taste of dust, and I try to avoid the broken vodka bottles as well as something that looks like desiccated human feces. My God, I think. What am I getting myself into, exactly? I must have lost my mind, letting myself get mixed up in the kind of thing the crime shows like to feature.

In the distance, splotches of diffuse light pulse.

HALF AN HOUR LATER, underslept and exhausted, I wander my environs. The ice is beginning to melt. I take off my duffle coat and on a wood platform by a pond teeming with cattails and grassweed I lie down gazing up at the clear blue sky. Above me, on the rough branch of a wild apple tree, a single apple dangles, reminding me of a certain forebear.

During the war, my grandfather Władek, along with some other riflemen from the infantry, wound up in the Lamsdorf Stalag in Łambinowice, near Opole, which the Nazis called the Briten lagen because since nineteen-forty they kept primarily British prisoners of war there. My grandfather got a tip about an upcoming dispatch to a concentration camp and so planned his escape. As a carpenter, he occasionally got a pass and went out for materials through the gate of the Stalag. Apparently, he took advantage to copy the keys, and he did escape, along with two English commandos. In the whole history of Lamsdorf, out of a hundred thousand inmates, only thirteen or fourteen managed to get free. The guards mostly shackled and chained the English soldiers, especially the airmen. My grandfather was one of the few who survived and was able to hide until the end of the war in the caves and dugouts around the Polish Jurassic Highland. I lived with him for eighteen years, and during that time I tried repeatedly to ask him questions about the war. In response, he would sing forbidden songs, but he would never talk about the Stalag, making it clear to me that talking about his adventures with the Allies was a punishable offense. One day I was sitting in an apple tree, eating up ripe paper apples, swinging my legs. My grandfather was just coming back from the quarry and noticed me sitting on my branch.

"Get down from there, you'll fall and then we'll be in trouble!" he shouted.

"I'm not coming down."

"Get down!"

"I'm not coming down."

"If you don't get down right now you'll get sent straight to Lamsdorf!"

"Lasdorf? Ladorf, la, do, fa," I mocked him, unaware of the significance of the word I was breaking apart.

ARE YOU THERE, LITTLE LADY? says my grandpa's voice. Can you hear me? I look around, there's no one there. On a branch over the swift stream of water that flows into the pond from some mysterious source, a dark-brown dipper flutters its wings. Would you come home already? Do you remember how I sowed that wheat? Now that you've gone off to that school of yours everything's been lying fallow. Your grandma in the grave, your mom alone don't have the strength for it. There's nobody left on our farms. They've all gone off into the cities. From ours, Lubasy, Władzia to Będzin, Ania to Siemianowice, and the boys off to the factories. But the youngest Zośka stayed, but she was taking two shifts at the plant doing those woven baskets. Even wet behind the ears she could help quarry, and with timber she was strong as though she weren't no girl, not like you, just sitting around all day with your nose in some book. Better off writing how nobody these days puts up pine crowns on the doorframes anymore, nobody puts anything up by the bridge when there's a wedding, nobody makes żurek, It's been three years now since the firemen brought a calendar. They used to give them out. You'd just give what you could for them, so long as it wasn't less than fifty zlotys. The milkman doesn't make his rounds no more, meanwhile there's nowhere to go and get a simple footstool now, and they went and opened up that inn in Koziegłów on the main little square there. We all had a good cry when they did that. Then they fixed the streets up. They said we lived on Długa. How could we live on Long Street, I ask the letter-carrier, when it's as stunted as it is? The kids saw too much television and got it into their heads to get rich off artificial Christmas trees, and bark, and florals, wreaths—and then everybody took the doors off the hinges to their houses and made arches just like in a chapel. But I'll tell you one thing: it wasn't the televisions made them stupid. Whether for the priest or the nobility, we never had any respect round here.

Once in thirty-nine this guy in Siewierz ratted me out for smuggling sausages. I must have had four kilos hidden in my pockets when all of a sudden out pops this Kraut pointing his Luger, wanting to know what I'm doing there on that cart, and I hardly think about it, I just say: *Trinken, essen und schlafen.* My God, the panic that got hold of me. And there that Kraut just bust out laughing. Ever since then I've always played the fool, whether it's church folk or party folk, I'd sign with a cross, although you've seen yourself how good I know how to write.

You wouldn't remember when your father Ryś got bumped from the paper mill, would you? Since he was the porter there, he was the one to open the gate up, and shut it, but I guess he'd leave it open a little too often. Soon as they got rid of him, he learned how to lay boards from a pal, and from that then on he could get away from work. Everybody had him do their bathrooms, and then they'd offer him some vodka at the end of the day. That's how the poor kid drank himself to death, his heart just wouldn't hold out.

But were you still here when the mayor invited the choir for the harvest festival? Kid, he brought these devil-worshippers into our town to perform at the, well, at the amphitheater. They called themselves the Nightingales, but they weren't even a choir, just some hooligans. And the way they played, kid, the way they let loose—well, it was like the drums of hell sounding off right here in Hektary. The kids all wailed, and the womenfolk ran home, and that was the end of our harvest festival. And then when you went off to that school of yours, these chicken farms started build-ing in Hektary, pipelines, and people were selling off their fields. Once up top the hill I even saw some people collect-ing snails into a cart. Even snails, you understand? Even snails they want to take away from us, gall darn it—what do they want them for? I'll hand them the snails, the quarry's crawling with them. And who knows who they plan on giv-ing those plots of land to. Sounds like it's through contacts. Once they started building on the priest's field and on those, you know, state farms, where the basements'd flood every so often, then I really did get scared, that just look, here come the Germans back to buy up all our land. Kiddo, that would be the end of days, or however you want to think of it, but if they took our fields from us. I've got pitchforks and an ax should anything arise.

From a nearby meadow a flock of crows takes off, bearing up some sapphire clouds along their wingtips. The shadows of the trees and rushes over the pond are getting longer. I sit on the platform, and recalling Natka's parcel, I take it out of my jacket pocket, examining the electrical tape that covers it completely. I sniff it; my internal struggle over whether or not to check to see what it contains rages on. Finally, however, I decide to leave it be and turn and go back to the shelter. When I get there, sleet is falling. The smoke from the chimneys slants to the west. I kneel at the entrance, which has been dismantled by scrap collectors, and pat the loose board. I'm trying to stuff the parcel underneath it when suddenly someone touches my shoulder. I jump, covering my face. Before me stands Scurvy, Natka Roszenko's old lover, who in my village in the eighties was the owner of Baboon, a nightclub by the side of the highway. He hasn't changed except for going slightly gray and shaving off his bushy mustache.

"You're alive?""

Scurvy blinks his bloodshot eyes and takes a good long look at me.

"How do you do, Ryś's kid." He smiles, puts a finger on his lips and jams the parcel into his briefcase.

I shuffle after him towards a cream-colored VW I've often seen parked in the drive of the Vega. I'm tired, so I'd rather ask no questions and not bring up Natka. A wooden rosary draped over the front mirror rocks rhythmically. The sound of the engine half puts me to sleep. I look out the window, where the trees delight me as never before: poplars, aspens, hornbeams, beeches making with their branches the discreet movements of clock hands. Stately and silent, they turn the surfaces of their leaves towards the setting sun, which for one split second clings to the hawthorn fruit, wild rose and bird cherry, until at last like a knot of hair tossed onto the hot surface of a stove it is extinguished completely.

"Do you ever see at the station this homeless geezer who just stares at the tracks and sings carols and gives out religious cards?" Scurvy stops the car by the train station and hands me a cigarette. I'm afraid to say no, so I take a reluctant drag.

"Yes, that guy does hang around here. I've seen him a couple of times," I answer shyly, coughing a little.

"That's Clod."

"You know him?"

"I gave him that nickname myself back in the clink in Herby, because—fittingly enough—he had this clod he'd dug up, and he was always singing carols at the station, you know."

"What was he in jail for?"

"Butter."

"What do you mean?"

"What I said. He was locked up for nothing, because he took something, out of hunger—I think it was a little bread, and because he had no place to live, and the law in our country is so fucked—pardon me—that if you don't got an address, then you go straight into captivity to await your case. At first he was in this other block, upstairs, but since he was slightly off—just the facts—he couldn't quite accommodate their rules there, so they threw him out. Meanwhile the chief officer in Herby was, no joke, Herbik."

"Herbik in Herby?"

"I'd hardly make it up, now would I?"

"Right."

"Herbik had things arranged with some butcher—brother-in-law, son-in-law, uncle, I don't know, but I do know that when I was in the hospital for some tests my food was seven times worse than it was in the can: a kilo of kielbasa for breakfast, another kilo for lunch. It got to where we couldn't even stand to see a sausage. But since Clod had been homeless for most of his life, he'd learned to put away some food for later, and he would keep his kielbasa in a pillowcase. It started to smell like you can't even imagine in his cell. We'd give him all sorts of things from the donations so he'd stop, but he'd still store his kielbasa in his pillowcase. We could never get him to quit—that was just the way he was.

"Clod would write in to the court every day, every letter of every word some two centimeters tall, like he was a child, pleading with this judge Ms. Ania Something-or-Other: "I did not do nothing, I did not do nothing," he'd write, and he'd slip in some religious card, with the Virgin Mary, you know, because of that's the way it is in Częstochowa. I thought I was a pretty tough cookie, like your pops, old Ryś, who fled the army and got half his unit onto a wild goose chase, but when I'd look at Clod my heart would really break into a million pieces. He was the only one of all of us who longed for freedom so bad he was capable of standing four, five hours without any break next to the window, staring out through the bars into the forest, the tracks and shouting how he wanted to go home. Home: the very thing he'd never had—and never would."

THE STREET RUNNING IN FRONT OF THE STATION starts to smell like chimney smoke and exhaust fumes. Anxious travelers pace it up and down. From the ground floor of the Polonia Hotel come the muffled sounds of an orchestra. Steam rises from drainage wells. The wind raises a shred of wrapper and flings it onto a wire sticking out from the fence. Scurvy takes his Centertel phone out of its black case and, chomping on a kebab, anxiously converses with someone. I glance at his tanned, unshaven face, and then at the platform: off scoots another train I could have taken home.

"I guess I'll take my leave now, Scurvy, sir. Thanks for the lift."

"Where are you rushing off to? It's not like I'm going to eat you," Scurvy laughs. "I wanted to give you your suitcase and tell you a little story about our mutual friend, Waldek. Do you know how he got his limp?"

"Nope."

"It was the hats and bats that did it."

"What are the hats and bats?" I sit down next to Scurvy on the bench.

"Easy there, easy. I'm about to take you through it step by step. Waldek was in the clink with me for some drunken brawl, and the whole time he wouldn't talk to anybody, unless he absolutely had to. He just went mute. He would read some old magazine on stars and moons and planets and periodically wake up in the middle of the night screaming, 'Adelka! Adelka!' Adelka had been living with Waldek and hanging around with this guy who had a mirror factory; two years she worked in his brothel on Mirowska Street."

"He told us about her, too."

"What a cunt. I would never have tolerated a woman like that . . ." Scurvy clears his throat and takes a swig from his flask. "Coming up to Christmas the guys and I were scheming on how to get some mash in here, to get some liquor going. Kind of a paste, you can make it out of tooth-paste and diazepam, sixty- to eighty-proof, but that would stink, and it wouldn't be too good, and we wanted some-thing better for ourselves. During visiting hours we would go to the canteen and get five-liter mineral waters, so we already had the bottles, that was a start of sorts, at least. Then we all got Danishes for Christmas, and none of us ate ours, we just stored them up, eager to ferment them. We sprinkled some sugar in there and took care of it like it was a child. We re-ally did. Wrapped them up in newspapers and blankets, kept them in back of the beds, but since there wasn't that little tube that would ventilate it, you had to take turns getting up every hour to take the plug out and release the gas so it wouldn't explode. Things went along like that just fine for about three weeks, us getting up to burp our little one, which had started to smell lovely like wine, when all of a sudden the goon squad comes into our cell for a shakedown. They rounded us up along with a cell of snot-noses . . ."

"Snot-?"

"Twenty-five-and-unders. So they round us all up and have us strip down completely so they can search us, and they check our shoes, our pants, have us squat and so on. They come up with nothing, so we start to go back. But the cells have been absolutely fucked, it's a real shambles in there: bread in the toilets, socks in the sugar. And basically we get that we are fucked because they found our hooch. Once and they hold our parcels, our visits, take away our TVs and so on, twice and they send in the hats and bats to fuck us up for real."

"What are the hats and bats, Scurvy?"

"The hats and bats are this special C/O unit that's kind of like urban counterterrorism or something. Mostly ex-ZOMO. They generally don't stick out too much because they're constantly sitting around just getting shit-faced. That's how it is, a habit from communist days. But whenever somebody presents a threat, they strap on their helmets, pick up their shields and their bats and open up the cells and storm in there six at a time and just beat the shit out of everyone. Anyone they come across, they fuck them up, they don't care. You go to try and smile and you find out you don't have any teeth left."

"Were you afraid of them?"

"Well, what do you think? Even the biggest thugs are scared of them. They've killed their share of guys, and afterwards they write it up like as though the poor guy hanged himself, or whatever, had a heart attack or something. But getting back to the hooch. So we're standing there butt naked. That dick Frania comes out of the condom—condom's what we called that ribbed C/O booth they had there—and he says, 'Gentleman, I'm gonna keep it short: if you don't tell me whose hooch this is, you're all fucked.'

"But we refuse to confess to anything. The snot-noses don't make any peeps, neither.

"'Gentlemen, this is the last time I'll ask, and if you don't answer me I'm calling the hats and bats, and all hell will break loose. Who brewed the hooch?'

"And that's when Waldek stood up, scratching at his chest because he's had scabies for ages, and he says:

"'It was me!'"

2.
Your Name's Anula Now

THE TRAIN STATION'S WAITING AREA is separated from the passageway by a wall of glass. In it frolic the flashes of arcade games. Guys in tracksuits put in their tokens and fire up The Punisher. The figures of the Terminator, Jungle King hanging from a vine and a red-hot Tekken fly across the screen.

I wander around the station and try and think where I could wait out the night. It's warmer than usual, and flu viruses are running wild. A southwest wind gusts against the station's glass roof, ferreting around the twenty-two pylons that hold the building up.

When it gets colder again, though, I take my suitcase and move into the snack bar, where I buy tea in a little plastic cup and sit at a little metal table, mesmerized by the contorted reflection of my hands. In the paper, under the new currency design with the portrait of Władysław Jagiełło, I read announcements for a German holding company, envelope addressing, tire retreading and the discrete young ladies of Monika & Co.

A tall man wearing glasses walks into the snack bar, orders tea and settles down next to me at my table.

"Can you gals believe what they've done to this station?"

The woman who runs this place looks him over and adjusts her unlacquered perm, releasing flurries of dandruff onto the counter. The reflecting triangles glued to the wall proliferate her heavily made-up face.

"I had—if you'll permit me—the pleasure of first encountering this station of ours during the era of the Warsaw-Vienna Railway," says the man and strokes his chin as an amber-colored droplet of tea makes its way down and onto his neck. "The old building had this little turret that resembled a locomotive in shape. It used to be a place with a fine attention to detail: little windows, light fixtures, the street lamps outside. In spacious restaurants around tables covered in white cloths, waiters wearing suits, bustling about." He closes his eyes for a moment, then gesticulates as though slides were being played in the triangular mirrors on the wall.

"I don't know why, but it used to smell more like brewed coffee than it did like food. Next door there was a hairdresser's, and I think it was even open at night. Oh, those were the days, my dears: trains, the whistles of the locomotives, smoke, steam that would hiss, the smell of grease and oil, commotion, the passengers' progress, people on pilgrimages, old broads from the country and big city dames, conductors and civic militia walking two by two, the straps from their caps dangling under their chins. I remember that over by Freedom Avenue passengers would just walk right out onto the tracks, where the conductor would stand in one designated place and check tickets. Back then tickets were like heavy cardboard tags."

"You're a regular Papa Smurf! That memory," jokes the snack bar attendant as she sets some cans of Coca-Cola in the fridge.

The man glances at her with a glint in his eye, fingers the skirt of his coat. "I recall it all, Madame, because in the late fifties and early sixties I would often travel by train with my mother to Krakow. For several years every two weeks she would take me to the ophthalmology clinic where I underwent a surgery to improve my sight. But I was an unlucky child. The surgery was not a success, and as a result, my view of the world is limited to that which I can glean through just one eye."

NEW YEAR'S EVE JINGLES take over the snack bar radio. The new year—1995, a time of privatization, acquisitions, cable TV, securities, the issuing of bonds, companies, investment firms, pyramid schemes and predicting the end of the world—bursts over Biegański Square. I retreat from all that, escape into the station's passageways, check out the waiting room, where I sit in a row of wooden benches and slip into a drowsy lethargy. Through the openwork backs of the benches seep spots of light that dart along the floor like tadpoles. The passengers' breaths condense in the air. For the second time since I arrived in Częstochowa I think about dropping out of college, which—aside from a couple of lectures in my class on Old Polish literature—I haven't gotten anything out of so far, think about not trying to find Kamil anymore, about going back to Hektary.

"What could you be doing all alone at the train station at this time of night?" says an older, rather hefty woman with a pageboy haircut. She's come out of nowhere; in astonishment I stare at her a moment: each element of her outfit appears to hail from its own individual era, from the faded maroon waterproof coat to the black combat boots to the plaid scarf to the ornate felt hat with the feather in it, worn aslant; and she smells like lavender soap, like my grandma. "Aren't you afraid to roam around all alone like this, at night?" Her solicitous tone feels artificial. There is something about her I find unsettling, and yet, I answer.

"It just sort of happened this way, Ma'am." I hide my hands, which are scraped up by blackberry bushes, in my pockets.

"You must be hungry," she says and proffers a sandwich wrapped in gray paper. "Did you just arrive in Częstochowa?"

"I've been in Częstochowa since the end of September. I just moved out of my previous accommodations in Sabinów, Ma'mmm," I try to say as I devour a slice of Mortadella: I've barely eaten all day, just wandering around since parting with Scurvy outside.

"Sabinów? Where the Russkies are stationed?"

"They're not stationed there anymore, it's just civilians who come to Poland for business."

"But how could you have ended up there?"

"I didn't get a spot in the dorms because my village is too close to Częstochowa, but since I wasn't going to be able to get cheap passes to take the train in every day, I rented those accommodations in a workers' residence."

I want to tell her about the Vega, about Natka, Waldek, Adelka, the Russians, but instead I merely mutter something about the workers' housing being so terriby cold, since there wasn't any heating.

"Good thing you got out of there, my dear!" She gives a sweeping wave: the wind is howling outside.

A spirited band of teens jolts down the passageway, toting half-full bottles of cheap sweet wine under their jackets, boasting of their recent heist of the contents of the alms box at the monastery in Jasna Góra. One of them, dressed up as an elf, leans out over the railing at the top of the stairs. His white pom-pom dangles over the precipice like a snowball.

"I'll fucking jump, I'll jump, and can't nobody stop me! Daria! Daria!" he screams out across all the station's premises, but when a city guard looks up from behind a partition, the teen shuts up, covers his face with the corner of his cap.

"I think we had better get out of here," the woman whispers.

"It's just . . . I don't have anywhere to go, Ma'am. I have to wait for my train here, till dawn."

"I can rent you a room in the attic of where we live."

I look at her intrigued, but without saying anything, knowing I've only got a few cents in my wallet.

"Listen, child, you can't wait in here all night alone. It isn't safe. I'm Mother Stanisława, an oblate from the Congregation of the Sisters in Christ's Heart."

"Oblate?"

"Like a nun, but without the habit," she says in a more familiar tone. "Just think, for some time I've been looking for a female student who might, in exchange for her accommodations, help me out with a few small domestic tasks." She reaches inside the pocket of her coat and hands me an apple covered in communion wafer crumbs, and then, without waiting for a response, she takes my suitcase and drags it out along the sidewalk towards a stand where, since it's New Year's Eve, there are no taxis.

NEW YEAR'S NIGHT IS ASTONISHINGLY WARM, and also rainy and windy. The street lamps dissolve into the mist like pears in the midst of leaves. In half-curtained windows, the twinkle of television screens. Paving stones glisten in the drizzle like snakeskin. Drunk girls clad in sequins clack along the sidewalk, inadvertently invoking the echoes of the city as it once was, when the streets were given rhythm by the trolleys and by horses' hooves. The wind ruffles the Fiat Punto ads stapled to the fence, lifts aloft the flyers for phone sex hotlines, those soaked to crumbling Xeroxes of virgins driven mad by passion, eager-to-please police ladies, cleverly treacherous wives.

We're standing near the stalls that sell French fries on Piłsudski Street, where even the tree bark has soaked up the scent of the frying oil. Finally our taxi drives up and squeals to a halt. A seemingly drunk driver squeezes out of it. He has the sloppy posture of Kokosz and after situating my suitcase in the trunk, he hurls himself onto the front seat with such force that the car literally sinks down to the cobbles. Glancing at us with his bloodshot eyes in the rear-view mirror, which also shows our own exhausted faces, he switches on the radio and starts singing, or more accurately, howling the latest hit by Varius Manx: "Don't be afraid to be afraid. When you feel like it, just cry. Go out and hunt down the wind." Peeling ourselves off of the beer-infused upholstery after being bounced back and forth, in first gear, from curb to curb, for twenty minutes, we finally get out near a church with a brick tower at the intersection of Saint Barbara and Saint Augustine Streets.

The last dregs of my energy leave me as we walk inside a plaster-coated compound separated from the street by an iron gate. Past that gate it's stuffy. My head is pounding. Flu pain clamps down on my muscles. Dragging my feet, I follow the oblate through the walled-in courtyard straight to the entrance to the convent. Thinking of Márquez's story "I Only Came to Use the Phone," which I had read in some literary journal before leaving home to come to college, I hesitate at the threshold of this order, but in the end I cross. We go through the vestibule and pass by another little booth, here inhabited by a porter woman. A woman the residents of this house call Mother Superior gives me a pair of wooden clogs and says I must absolutely wear them when I walk about the convent, then gives me a few further instructions. The sisters buzz around me like bees, collecting my soaked clothes and my boots that are too big for me that Ludmila gave me in the morning. Then they redress me in a linen nightgown and invite me down to the refectory, where a steaming krupnik, sprinkled with fresh dill, awaits.

When I finish eating, the Mother Superior makes me drink a bitter herbal infusion that reeks of black elderberry, fungus and cat pee, then leads me up the stairs to the attic, kicks aside the dried Advent wreaths sprawled across the doormat, and, cracking a door with the number eleven on it, she motions for me to go inside. In the warm, clean room, the roof creaks like a moored ship, the bedding smells like wind and starch, and the light green satin bedspread ripples like winter rye.

AFTER SO MANY INTERRUPTED NIGHTS at the Vega, the Congregation of the Sisters of Christ's Heart seems like an oasis of peace. I quickly grow accustomed to the heavy clogs I have to wear on convent property, to the early-morning wakeups, the canonical hours from matins to vespers, the vegetarian dishes consisting primarily of buckwheat porridge, fermented milk, peas, beans, żurek and cabbage.

Dressed up in the mandatory uniform of the oblate— a loose blouse and skirt that has to be below the knee—I humbly carry out the orders of the Mother Superior, written out in ink on a special card I find every morning under the door to my room in the attic. My duties include: mopping and polishing the floors in the tourist wing; washing the holy figurines with warm water and dish soap; cleaning the confessionals in the chapel, where a priest comes in to take the sisters' confessions; preparing two dozen bottles for the healing water that comes from Saint Barbara's Cathedral's little holy spring; and helping out with all the smaller tasks.

At first the sisters—who are used to the perpetual short-lived visits of the pilgrims to whom they rent rooms at any time of day or night—regard me with a certain wariness, as a stranger who has suddenly shown up in their home and now eats in their refectory and drinks from their mugs and—worst of all—sleeps in the guest room in the attic, which is supposed to be reserved for curia higher-ups.

But as I meekly wash the plaster statues, polish the floors and peel potatoes, the sisters begin to accept me; they talk with me in the hallways, share preserves, pass down holy pictures, herbal mixtures and whatever treats get left behind in the rooms rented by pilgrims from the West. And so I get to know Zyta, who is the Mother Superior's right hand—although in fact she seems to run the whole convent; Sabina, the cook, who comes from Bytom and who, like my aunt, used to work in a mine canteen when she was younger, making the tastiest soups in all of Silesia; Sister Basia—short for Barbara—who plays violin in the chapel and who, like her namesake—Saint Barbara—is an only child and ran away from home in her youth, jokingly referring to her father as Dioscorus since, like Saint Barbara's father, he wanted to keep her imprisoned in a tower on his estate, built on a post-Soviet field. And yet I have the most to talk about with the youngest oblate, Sister Anna, who lives next to the library, is around forty years of age, and like me studied languages and letters. Whenever I hear her clogs tapping out iambs on the staircase, I hurriedly tidy up my room, toss the green bedspread over the bed and wait for her to come like a child expecting Santa Claus.

Then Sister Anna comes into my room. As we sip our tea, we stretch out comfortably atop the bed like teenaged girls at summer camp. Sister Anna tells me about her great-grandmother, who had five children and ran a pharmacy by the train station and who died in thirty-nine from the one bomb that fell on Częstochowa.

Late into the evening she reads me poems by Narcyza Żmichowska, Julian Ejsmond's *The Lives of Trees*, Henryk Zwierzchowski's sonnets about his granddaughter from *The Garden of Life*, until at some point, she falls asleep.

Quiet as a mouse I venture out into the bathroom, where I change into my pajamas, and then I lie down beside her along the edge of the bed, listening to her soft breaths, examining the skylight, its glistening patterns, embroidered by the frost.

My birthday is on the ninth of February, but I don't mention it to the sisters. Since I have tonsillitis I spend the whole break in the convent. I lie feverish in bed, waking up and falling back asleep, listening to Paganini's caprices for violin, which Sister Basia plays in the chapel.

Just before Lent, Sabina, the cook, looks in on me, fluffs up my pillows and offers me some angel wings, which she has fried in lard. At one point, she goes up to the nightstand and picks up the little pot with the Mother Superior's herbal infusion in it.

"Ew, girl, this stinks to high heaven. I would not drink this if it were me," she says in horror, then leaves.

I pour the Mother Superior's infusion into the toilet and immediately feel better, and then when Sister Anna brings me ampicillin capsules from a doctor friend of hers, I recover fully. As I snack on the wafers I found overnight in the common room of the convent's tourist wing, I read Klemens Janicki's *Meditations*. Under that lyrical influence, my thoughts return to my grandfather Władek. My mom wrote me that he had the flu, too, and that he wasn't doing very well. "He keeps switching from one end of the bed to the other, sure that as long as the Grim Reaper only hovers over the headboard, rather than going down to the foot, a person still has hope."

I go down the hill with my grandfather; we pass the forest and the dolostone mine. It all looks familiar. Our little hill, the barn, the outhouse, the stoneware, the cherries, our juniper. Dogs run around the square, but they don't come up to us, don't bark and don't growl. They don't seem to notice my grandpa. Has he already died? I remember that before I left he asked me for a new hat. I measured his gray head with a ribbon, but since the last day of last September, I haven't gone home. Now guilt peals in my ears.

The next day, in honor of the approaching Week of Prayer for the Sobriety of the Nation, at Sister Zyta's behest, I outline and cut out the cardboard letters that, when tacked to their wooden slats, will make up the principle pronouncement of that apostle of sobriety, the Venerable Matt Talbot: "May today's world, so absorbed by sensuality, learn how to properly mortify the body."

ON MY RETURN FROM MY LECTURE on descriptive grammar, halfway along Saint Barbara Street, I peek inside one of the ruined, cluttered outbuildings, where I watch with a smile as children collect ladybugs on a burdock leaf, count the dots on their wings, prepare in emptied cans sorrel and daisy soup spiced with sand or swing on tires. By seven their mothers show up outside, coming down the brick steps, calling them for dinner, taking down from clotheslines laundry permeated by the definite chill in the air.

When the courtyard empties fully and starts to smell like cocoa and boiled wiener sausages, I get hungry and turn back to the main street, heading towards Saint Barbara's Cathedral, its copper spire delicately piercing two clouds that are slowly evanescing into night. I pass shop windows scrubbed clean in preparation for Easter, glance at the orange sign of the clergy supply store Temporis. Old blooming trees drenched in spring light seem to cleanse the street, stop time. I run my fingers over their warm bark, their rough boughs and hanging twigs. Spring has taken hold of more than just the city. As buds burst into bloom, my yearning for Kamil intensifies, gets more physical, hurts, throbs in every cell of my body. His face has transformed in my memory and is nobler.

In the end, exhausted, I make it to the Congregation of the Sisters in Christ's Heart. I pass through the iron gate and put on my clogs. In the empty refectory I leaf through a newspaper left on the table and read an ad encouraging childless women who love nature between the ages of eighteen to forty to go to Austria, Switzerland or Bavaria. It's been circled in black marker. For dinner I have buckwheat porridge with kefir, then I wash my dishes and hole up in my little attic room. After bathing, sipping the infusion of medicinal herbs made by the Mother Superior, I gaze up at the skylight; behind it, a seething ocean. Before I go to sleep, having thought once more of Kamil's face, I read the instructions for my descriptive grammar homework, go back over the first conjugation for my Latin class and crack the window to air out the stuffy room.

The meowing of mating cats sounds like newborns crying, or like a riveting rendition of the Song of Songs.

AFTER BREAKFAST OF RICE PUDDING made by Sister Sabina, I put on a dark green linen dress with slender straps, a wooden pendant and some sandals and exit the convent to wander the heart of Częstochowa in the hopes of catching sight of Kamil in the crowd. All the mannequins in all the boutiques look back at me with his eyes. Meandering up and down HVM Ave, I stare passersby's faces. Will I even recognize him after all these months? Though couldn't he have left town by now? Sometimes I think I see him outside the Franke House at the intersection of First Avenue and Wilson Street, by the observatory in Staszic Park, on Solidarity Square by the sculpture of buxom Mrs. Kowalski, supposedly installed on the orders of a party secretary named Mr. Kowalski; I look in the window of the Żyrafa, of the Orbis. But he isn't ever anywhere.

The heat reaches its apogee, and I can smell melting asphalt. I sit on a bench and stare at the Cepelia building; the colorful round stones that encrust its façade glisten in the sunshine like trout scales. The sidewalks are littered with the remains of balloons, golden everlastings, ferns and evergreens from harvest festival wreaths, as well as pennants with the symbols of parishes from all over Poland.

"Our book works for you," says a man who, in such broad daylight, looks like the devil's legal representative. Despite the heat, he's dressed in a black suit and a synthetic silk tie. "It works for you three hundred and sixty-five days a year, twenty-four hours a day, and it truly is everywhere," he recites hoarsely.

Assuming he's referring to some new collection of apocrypha, I reach out to receive whatever it is. Sweating and smelling of Brutal cologne, this devil's lawyer reaches into his attaché case, hands me a phone book and vanishes around the corner just as suddenly as he first appeared in my field of vision. I cover my head with the yellow tome and remain seated on the bench until finally a band of pilgrims from Żytomierz with a crumpled banner that reads "Children of Ukraine" emerges from Third Avenue. Some patron of first aid greets them with saline drips. Bored, I drag myself off the bench and take a look around the reading room, where I look for articles in the papers about Częstochowa's Bloody Monday for a few hours, at the Mother Superior's request.

When I leave the library I put on my sunglasses, which makes me feel safer, and I wander the city center almost till nightfall, feeling strangely feverish, stumbling into people, shadows and birds that swoop down from the roof of the town hall straight to my feet. I pass a bakery that smells like Napoleonkas, the Lee Cooper on the corner, then walk to Biegański Square, which used to be called Magistracki Square; it was there in the earliest days of the war—on Monday, September fourth, nineteen thirty-nine—that hordes of people spent hours on end lying face down on the ground.

"It was maybe eight or nine o'clock in the evening," says the woman I meet walking around by the town hall. "We were just at home. It was my father, brother, and, you know, my mother and I with the baby, because my husband had gone off to the war. We had no lights on in the house—you weren't allowed to. A lot of the neighbors had fled already, but my father didn't want to because there'd been this neighbor who—well, she kept on saying, you needn't run away, there's no one going to hurt you. And my father, well, he heeded her, while the rest of them all fled. Like my other brother, ran off into the fields, up into the Kawie Mountains—they lay down there in the potatoes clear till morning, but my father wouldn't run away. My father wouldn't flee. I began to hear gunfire coming from Warsaw Street, and then they came for us. They went into all the apartments, when they were locked they just beat down the doors with the butts of their armaments, tore through locks, that's how they conducted their searches. They led us all out into the street, which was full of automobiles. They lined up two hundred men under the window, while we women had to go under the other, on the other side. I was holding the baby, my son, who was about to be a year old on September twenty-first. I got up to my father, and I say to him: Dad, where are you going? And he says, How would I know, child? How can I know? They drove us all outside, locked the gates. They kept us there and kept us there, with our hands in the air, up against the wall. They had their machine guns—then this older one took out this piece of paper and read something in German to us, and at one point he said: Heil, Hitler. The army said it after him, and that's when he gave the order. My father was wounded and fell down to the ground, but my brother and all of those other ones were killed. Then the Germans went to their vehicles, but one of them turned around and threw in a grenade, and that grenade took care of my dad . . . You went up to look at him after that, and it was . . . My God, and when I saw my poor brother, just lying there like that. Of course we were the ones who had to bury them, but all we had to do it with was our own two hands. That evening everything burned, everything but everything, burned . . ."

Now I take a look around the city. Small balloons knocked around by the wind rock over the pavement. Older people doze off under parasols. Tipsy bandaged pilgrims in straw hats, looking preposterous with neckerchiefs affixed to their heads, trail around the monastery, the baths at the Pilgrim House and the stations of the cross. In the underground passageways volunteers give out water and condoms; pickpockets, religious fanatics and prostitutes divvy up their beats. Jehovah's Witnesses, carrying old issues of *The Watchtower*, announcing the latest upcoming apocalypse. Younger pilgrims, clustered in and around the pavilions, gazebos and places to grab a bite like Prasowa or Wakans or Alex, hum "Abba Father" and peruse the twenty-four-hour liquor stores and the drug dealers, who come to Jasna Góra in droves during pilgrimage season. I sit atop a low wall and, without taking off my sunglasses, I stealthily touch the hot concrete with my palm. The city swells with the cacophony of guitars, harmonicas and drums, but beneath that surface rest layers of silence, pulse underground rivers, only barely making themselves known, as though the ground were a kind of forgetting.

AFTER THE CALL OF JASNA GÓRA, with dusk encroaching, I speed up my step, cut across Staszic Park and tread carefully between the bodies of pilgrims numbed by alcohol and deep asleep, lying on benches and mats placed under trees as though they'd just finished fighting some tough battle.

Once I pass the tiny stores with devotional articles along Seven Tenements Street, I turn left, onto Saint Barbara, which drops steeply to Kazimierz Street, rising again slightly only to fall once more towards the Cathedral. I linger among the rows of wooden stalls, deserted at this time of day, littered with popsicle sticks and broken parasols and tinsel and bottles and cards for "Mercantile Mercury" with a timetable of August pilgrimages.

I've made a new friend who hangs out at one of these stalls, a gregarious rat I call Rydzyk, like the milk-cap mushroom, because his coat changes color depending on the light: sometimes he looks reddish gray, other times just brown. Behind a scrap of something hanging, in that darkness, Rydzyk's little eyes now gleam like phosphorescent grains. When he detects my scent, he runs down a beam straight onto my hand and stares at me stubbornly, just waiting for me to break up some bread for him, part of one of the obwarzanki or the Kaiser rolls I get from a woman I know who sells them. I kiss Rydzyk on his tiny twitching whiskers, set him on my shoulder and sit down on the steps of the annex, right outside the pharmacy, where in the red light of an ad for some heart medication I remove my mascara, take off my earrings and tie my hair back into a ponytail so that I can return to the convent as the school-girl version of myself. I put Rydzyk down in the courtyard next to a trash can, open the door and watch him for a moment as he zigzags back towards the stalls like a brownish leaf driven by the wind. A golden glow pulsates in the windows of the dormitory. The iron gate is locked. I'm afraid to use the entry phone—I wouldn't want to wake the sisters—so I toss my backpack in between the bars and climb up the gate, which is topped in what looks like the bars of a gridiron. Alerted by the noise, the porter woman glances out and sees me hanging from the enclosure.

"This is the last time I'm letting you come in this late," she says, wagging a finger at me through the little window of her booth as I creep inside the convent.

"Please forgive me, sister." I look at her imploringly, begging her internally to please not rat me out.

"This had better be the last time, or I'll tell the Mother Superior about all of it."

"Thank you."

"Now get up to the attic."

"Yes, ma'am!" I say, eager as a team captain, and I

grab my clogs from behind the statue of Saint Barbara and start to tiptoe up the stairs. But on my way I come across a weeping mother superior, sitting on the floor, slumped against the door to her office.

"Is something the matter, Mother?" I ask, alarmed, trying to lift her.

"Sister Basia . . ." she tries to say, swallowing tears. "There won't be any music anymore, my child. Our Basia is no more . . . She always took such good care of herself . . ."

ON THE FIFTEENTH OF AUGUST, Blessed Green Virgin Mary Day, I spend the whole morning washing the confessional in the chapel with Ludwik detergent, then I throw my rag into a corner and sit on a bench by the door to the refectory, near the door's frame, which is decorated with evergreen and wildflowers, and I patiently await my turn, eavesdropping on the sisters as they debate important convent matters, as the convent fills with the smell of Sister Sabina's broth. It's a blend of scents: bay leaves, leeks, celery, allspice, lovage, parsley, lightly charred onions, pepper; their resounding grinding always reminds me of my grandmother Stefania. In August of 1979, as a five-year-old, I was barely tall enough to see what was on the table, but all the same I knew how to milk a cow, peel potatoes and make soup. My grandma would call me into the barn and have me stand by the chaff cutter and turn the crank as hard as I could. The gears would turn as in a music box, and then the chaff would fall into the basket and onto my bare feet, attaching to my cream-stained and blackberry-stained clothing. Dust and husks would swirl in shafts of sun. I'd lay more and more bundles of straw down on the wooden bed, and the chaff cutter would swallow them, creaking thrilled as a cradle swung into motion. That made me happy, too, and I always felt honored that my grandmother would spend so much time with me. Of course, what I understood then as playing in the barn with Grandma I later understood to be an important part of my training to work on the farm.

The mother superior calls me into the refectory. I sit down across from her at the table and stare at the plate of steaming broth with noodles.

"Go on, eat, just don't forget," she says with an enigmatic look.

"Bless us, O Lord, and these, Thy gifts," I recite, thinking she means I mustn't forget to say a prayer before my meal. "Through Christ, our Lord . . ."

"Anula!" she interrupts me excitedly, calling me by a name that isn't mine as she sets a little case with a ribbon tied around it on the table. "Surely you haven't forgotten it's your birthday today?"

I look up at her in some alarm.

". . . Amen," I say, and I take a deep breath. Then I venture: "Mother, my birthday is in February."

"I'm in no mood for teasing now, child—go ahead and unwrap it."

Reluctantly I pull the ribbon undone and peer into the case, where I find a gold ring with a cameo set in its center.

"God bless, Mother, but I can't accept this."

The mother superior leans in over the table and pushes the ring onto my finger.

"Now. Why don't you tell me why you went to the Grand Café today?"

"Grand Café? I don't know where that is. I'm sorry, I don't really know my way around Częstochowa quite yet."

"So what were you doing all day, then?"

"I spent the morning in the reading room, and then I went for a walk."

"I know, I know, my child, you don't want to talk about it, or you can't, but by God, if you really have to keep seeing that Leon, then don't go to the Grand Café, it's crawling with Volksdeutsche."

I cough, choking, it having hit me at last that the Mother Superior must be having trouble with her memory, just like my grandmother did.

"You'd better hurry up and get done with your food, you'll have to head to your lessons with Idzikowska in a minute."

Sister Zyta appears in the doorway of the refectory and signals to the Mother Superior that it is time for vespers. Once the Mother Superior, muttering curses or teachings under her breath, has left the refectory, Sister Zyta comes up to me, leans onto the table and, noticing the gold ring with the cameo on my finger, gives me a hard slap in the face.

"I would advise you, you sniveling beast," she hisses, "to get out of this place before it's too late. Just leave Mother Stanisława in peace."

"But . . ."

"Don't interrupt me when I'm talking to you. I know

perfectly well you've been provoking her, bringing up the war for no reason."

"I didn't do anything, Sister, I promise." My face is on fire. "It was the Mother Superior herself who always started the conversations, telling me about a husband and a pharmacist brother-in-law—I swear!"

"Quiet, you ungrateful brat! Your tongue will break out in hives when you lie like this, are you aware? Is this how you repay the Mother Superior for taking you in, taking you under her roof? She went through so much during the war. Do you understand?"

Instead of responding I stare at the silver cross that glitters over her neck like a molted mayfly, its nymph self lost.

WHEN I GET BACK UP TO THE ATTIC, I throw the satin bed-spread on the floor, and just to spite Sister Zyta, who inspects room several times a week—looking for pills or cigarettes or anything that might give her a pretext to throw me out of the convent—I lie down in my clogs on the clean sheets. My cheek is still burning.

I'm a few years old and don't know how to hide, how to protect myself. Everyone is stronger than me, they brandish their hands as though they'll wrench out pieces of me and keep them for themselves. My father calls me a changeling, a horrid changeling—words I can't quite understand, just like I don't get why, over the break, after the parish fair, he beat me with his army belt until I started bleeding. Maybe I messed up, maybe I did something I wasn't supposed to like scattering his bobbers, or maybe he did it out of a fear that he might have told me his secret while he was drunk? My grandma beats me just because—with a rag, a switch, anything she happens to run across—because of dementia, because of hypothyroidism. My teacher hits me on the knuckles with a ruler, or on the palms, because she hates her job. The boys stick their legs out to trip me, hit me with sticks, grope me in the boiler room at school, smash snow into my face on the playing field before our classes start because I'm just a little girl, defenseless. Only my grandpa, who must have killed people during the war, seems to have no intention of striking anybody now. He just takes his pickaxe, spade and shovel and goes and hides away in the quarry behind the barn, where—covered from head to toe in mud and dust—he spends hours extracting limestone. My mom, seething with resentment—over my father's outbursts, over the tragic death of her beloved older sister, over her life—hits me the most, because of anything and everything I do that angers her. One afternoon she notices a louse on my collar and hits me so hard in the back that I stumble into the hot stove. I'm too young to understand and start to think that since I am a horrid changeling that means that my blood is sweet, which is why the lice are breeding in my hair, so I start cutting my hands with pieces of glass. My mom, believing these wounds are accidental, pours hydrogen peroxide on them, sometimes a salicylic acid solution with ethanol, which burns, and then she bandages me up and kisses me on the cheeks and rubs my shoulders, heats up some water, and scrubs my head for me in clouds of steam. Then she uses a thick comb to get the lice out of my hair and onto a newspaper, where she crushes them with her fingernail over the dignitaries' bald heads. When she notices that I still have nits in my hair, that the combing has been insufficient, she takes the bike from the barn and rides four kilometers to the township, where there's a pharmacy, where she buys a solution that stinks like the pesticide we use on potato beetles, and she smears it into my unruly hair, wraps my head up in a kerchief and tells me to sit in the attic wearing that uncomfortable turban for the rest of the day. My head itches and burns. I play hide-and-seek with the cat, draw pictures on the dusty floor with my fingers, put together a mosaic out of shards of broken mirror and look under the tarpaulin where there are earwigs scampering around, apples rotting, celadon oat sprouts coming up. Hanging on lines to dry are clothes that smell of Pollena and my grandma's herbs: mint, sage and tansy. In bundles of poppy heads shades of green, violet and cerulean are gradually extinguished. Mother doves dive down into their hatchlings' little throats.

Suddenly, from behind an empty barrel, thrust into my field of vision by a beam of light, bursting, belted by a red tape like a chamberlain, a sack of wheat's appeared.

"Changeling, changeling!" whisper the poppy heads.

"Chay-chay ling, chay-chay ling," repeat the mother doves.

I hop from one leg to the other, swaying, like a puppy deafened by a shovel, then I grab a metal rod and, remembering all the blows, all the beatings, all the times, the wrenching, the spanking, I pound the sack so long that finally the burlap bursts. Through the opening in it escapes a golden stream of grains.

AT NINE, THE BELLS OF THE JASNA GÓRA APPEAL remind me of the Mother Superior's latest assignment. Inhaling the lightly dizzying scent of the adhesive from the strips of tape with which the cardboard boxes are assembled, I put out on the table the pink and blue plastic bottles that imitate the figure of Saint Barbara, which the sisters call Baby Marys. It's so quiet in my room I can hear the doves skipping around on the roof.

I put crown-shaped caps on the bottles and stick on labels with the convent's logo, continuing my work for such a long time that I produce a veritable pink and blue army of Baby Marys, standing ready to attack in two rows on the table. I crack the window. Hot air rushes in, blows over their bellies. The Kryk bakery, which does great business during pilgrimage time, emits rich and delicious scents.

I run down the stairs straight into the basement, where the convent's storeroom is. I find the door ajar. I take a peek inside. In a dark corner, by the plastic-wrapped artificial Christmas tree, glimmers the tip of Sister Anna's kerchief.

"God bless, Wioletta, I see you've forgotten the bottles again. I'm just doing inventory and put out your assignment by the door so that you wouldn't have to look for them."

"Bless you, sister."

My tired eyes peruse the two boxes with the carefully calligraphied WR11.15.08.1995: my initials, Wioletta Rogala, my room number and today's date.

"Doesn't it seem odd to you, Sister, that the Mother Superior spends so much time writing out all these numbers on our boxes?" I ask.

"Maybe she gets bored, or I don't know, maybe it calms her down to do it," she replies thoughtfully, then sits down on the newspapers in the corner of the storeroom. "Tada! Look what I have!" She takes out a tin of chocolates from under her apron: cat tongues, in German packaging.

"*Katzenzungen*! Sounds delightful." I sit down beside her on top of a box of wafers.

"The mother superior would beg to disagree." She smiles and winks conspiratorially at me.

Relishing the taste of chocolate, which I haven't had since Christmas, I think about my grandfather, who hated the German language as much as the Mother Superior does, and once more I turn my gaze to the numbers written on the cardboard boxes, imagining I've suddenly found myself inside a labyrinth with imprisoned women who can only ever escape by cracking these symbols' mysterious code. Some numbers seem to repeat, appearing in chains of sorts, in ciphers. Perhaps they're important dates from the Mother Superior's life.

"Are you still drinking those herbs?" asks Anna unexpectedly. "You've been looking a little frail lately," she adds, peering into the pale skin of my face. "You've got some inflammation at the corners of your lips and dark circles under your eyes. Maybe we should take you to a doctor?"

Instead of answering, I look at the watch wrapped around her slim wrist.

"Oh my, it's so late. I have to go, Sister, or I won't finish the Baby Marys for tomorrow. Good night."

"Nighty night, nighty night, don't let the bed bugs bite," she says, then quickly recites a stanza from a ballad by Narcyza Żmichowska:

> Oh! but beware!, oh! but beware—that sorceress
> Enchanting and delighting you with songs and sounds
> Is already flying so close and obscuring the stars,
> Tearing your heart out, devouring your soul.

Thinking about Kamil, I masturbate for a long time, so long it hurts. I grasp onto my forearms and thighs and leave bruises. The bruised tissue takes on different hues, loses its transparency, which lets me recover for some time the body I preferred to forget just a few years ago. Without turning on the light I wander through the convent, peeking into all the nooks and keyholes. I know that in these dormitories, so suffused with the fragrances of liquid wax and floor polish and incense, painful secrets lurk. I linger at the Mother Superior's cabinet, turn the golden knob and step inside. Candlesticks crusted over with wax, nib-carved, ink-stained notches extrude locks of hair of various colors, crumpled breviary pages, empty metallic candy wrappers. On the polished desk stands a gilded frame with a photograph of a young girl. Overwhelmed, I sink down onto the chair. That must be her! She is my mirror image, down to the light-colored curls and the freckles on her cheeks. I take the portrait in my hands: So you're her Anula? I take the elastic band out of my hair and look at my reflection in the glass, trying to wear my hair the same as Anula, parted in the middle. I glance around at the paintings hanging over the desk. All saints with pastoral scenes, scepters, skulls, lilies, miters, palms and peacock feathers seeming to lean out of their gilded frames, as though wanting to run away, up to the top of Jasna Góra, to the bergfried of the ruins of the Olsztyn Castle or to the Błeszno TV tower on that outlying hill.

Next to the folders with invoices on the desk I find, marked in ink and wrapped in plastic, a newspaper clipping that features a photo of a woman with blond hair. Margot Pietzner, married name Kunz, was an SS-Aufseherin at Ravensbrück until April 1945. After the war, she was arrested and sentenced by a Soviet military court and spent eight years behind bars. When she got out of jail, she took advantage of a unification agreement to apply for damages for the years she spent in prison and was granted compensation in the amount of sixty-four thousand Western marks. My eyes linger over an ad for Felix nuts in the lower right-hand corner, next to the article, the nuts' producers luring potential customers with the prospect of five marks' winnings in select cans. The juxtaposition surprises me, turns the ad into something more like a *Częstochowa Courier* PSA: "The brooms are here—let's turn out the lights at the office." I remember hearing the words "Margot, you bitch!" Did I hear those words? Where? Tromping nervously in my clogs over the parquet floor I go from wall to wall and back again, as though trapped in a dark cell. Finally, unable to remain any longer in this space so saturated with strangers' voices, where the clock beats like Giordano Bruno's heart and fantasies of the future take on vibrant shades, I cover my ears with my hands and run furiously out of the office, not knowing whether I hid my tracks behind me, whether I turned that golden knob, whether I even shut the door. I pass through the narrow entryway to the common room in the tourist wing of the convent, where as usual I go to the fridge and eat up the leftovers I find that foreign pilgrims have left behind or forgotten. I spit the half-chewed packaging from some cheese spread into the trash and, staring into the empty refrigerator, struggle internally over whether or not to again drink half a bottle of Maggi, or vinegar, or to eat the rest of the butter or a dry crust of bread. But at last I calm down and go back up to the attic.

With the photograph of Margot's face still vivid in my mind, I can't sleep. Mosquitos buzz rhythmically, as though copulating. I sink into the August night, into some intoxicating thing, jasmine-caramel, that won't let me sleep. I shudder under the covers and feel something taking root inside me. Shreds of others' memories and words effect certain changes. I remember that day when, plucking cherries, I accidentally knocked my ladder against a wasp nest. I was positioned near the top of the tree, tossing ripe, almost black fruit into my bucket. Suddenly, my thighs, shoulders, arms were riddled with such searing stings that it was as if someone were shooting at me with an air gun or burning me with a cigarette. The enraged wasps stung me again and again. Crazed with pain and fear, I let go of the ladder and fell from its highest rung right onto the nettles that surrounded the row of cherry trees that grew near the limit of the field. I got up in agony and ran home, where my grandma rubbed fermented milk into my stings. At night from stress or an overdose of venom I ran a high fever. In my dreams, as I broke through the white wasp nest and took hold of something that looked like glass wool, I saw them, my dead: my recently deceased grandpa Władek, my grandma Salomea from Sosnowiec, whom I only know from a portrait since her heart gave out long ago, my grandma Stefania, my grandpa Stanisław, my aunt Ania, my godfather Józek, uncles and aunts; I recognized them with some other sense, though they no longer had faces or individual features. That force, one emerged from many, a kind of quagmire.

"Sink into us! Come on! Come in!" they whisper, until finally spring starts here, though after a fleeting warming period, a frost cuts off the thaw, transforming the meadows around our stone house into a mosaic of shattered mirrors. Abruptly all my relatives exit one by one, and when they haven't come back into the room after a long while, I look for them in the entryway, in all the rooms, in the attic; I go over to the door to see if they might be outside, in the yard, but I can't cross the threshold. Finally I grow wings like bladder cherry leaves and fly out into the courtyard, where a fire burns in the center. There is a stench of smoldering tires, burnt hair, and skin. She, Margot Kunz, comes out of the shed—a charming salesgirl recast in the forties as executioner. Under the watchful eye of Maria Mandel, she excelled at her training for the concentration camp.

Those empty eyes, of uncertain color; the dark brows penciled into lovely arches; the light, sensitive complexion, somewhat broken out; the delicate neck with prominent hickeys; a ring on her finger. A pleasant voice, low; strong calves; little feet. She straightens her uniform, fastens the button at her neck and flashes me a smile. At that sight I leap into the flames.

AFTER LUNCH—Sister Sabina has prepared lazanki with mushrooms and sauerkraut—I return to my room, putting the latch in the hook behind me. I open the wardrobe and take out from the secret compartment in my suitcase an *Urania* of Waldek's, which over the course of my many-month stay at the convent has managed to absorb the aromas of incense, wax, and lavender moth cubes.

"On temperate evenings," I read, "as Saint Jerzy plays the violin, it's so entrancing that any living person who happened to listen would die right away of an excess of emotion. But in general such sinful creatures never get to hear these songs. Only occasionally a baby, asleep in the cradle, may suddenly smile in the night; the parents are unable to explain such infant bliss, yet it is a sign that the child has managed to hear, through a dream, the songs of highest Heaven. For innocent children have the gift of seeing extraordinary things; according to Jewish tradition, they are able to understand the speech of fire, of animals, of the wind, and of ghosts. Adults, however, cannot even look upon the Moon as Saint Jerzy plays, for if they do his strings might snap, blinding the erstwhile viewer."

Suddenly a metallic sound like the impact of a mallet on the bars of a xylophone carries across the courtyard. I look out the little open window. The moon clings to the tower on Jasna Góra like a bracket fungus to a birch trunk. A man's shadow gets longer on the asphalt. Just past the hedge his leather jacket flashes. I can't believe it. It's him, it's Kamil! I've been looking for him for so many months, and now he's here, right outside the iron gate. He looks exactly as he did in Hektary. He's standing on the street, trying to signal something. I throw my clogs into the corner and, heart pounding, in just my pajamas, I race barefoot downstairs. I wait a moment in the hallway and then, taking advantage of the porter's bathroom break, I press the orange button on the console. The entrance opens. I pass through the vestibule and with feet clapping against the concrete of the courtyard I run to the iron gate, where I can smell gasoline, oriental cologne, and tobacco. I'm near tears. I seize the bars in my hands. In the August air the metal loses density. At first I can't understand Kamil's words, which he pronounces quickly and chaotically. Only after a while do shreds of sentences finally reach me:

"Forgive me, forgive . . ." He kisses my hand.

"What could I possibly have to forgive you for?"

"Everything. I've only just returned to Częstochowa."

"Did you move away?"

"I go every so often to see my mother, who is ill, in Katowice."

"I was a little worried about you when you stopped coming to Hektary."

"What about you, are you okay?" he asks, staring into the V of my pajama top, which reveals a sliver of my firm little breast. "You've gotten very thin, Wiola, since the last time I saw you. Are you ill? Is that why you're hiding in this strange convent?"

"No, no, I'm fine," I say in a trembling voice. "I'm just renting a room from the sisters here, in the attic. It's a long story. I'll tell you all about it someday."

"I was worried."

"How did you find me?"

"I was at your house several times. I finally got your grandpa to give me your address."

"My grandpa?" I ask. Wresting any information out of that old coot borders on the miraculous.

"Oh, don't think it was easy." He smiles. "First I had to feed him half a liter of vodka."

We must be talking too loud, because the light in the vestibule of the convent flickers, filtering out through the window into the courtyard along a faltering path. We hear the door slam. Someone slowly comes down the stairs, clacking the convent's clogs against the concrete, getting closer and closer to us.

"I'm sorry," I say, "but there are no guests allowed at this hour."

"I understand, of course—I didn't even tell you I was planning to drop by. Come to Staszic Park tomorrow at four. I'll be waiting by the fountain." He blows me a kiss and moves behind the wall.

"Who's there?" I hear the resounding voice of the Mother Superior.

"It's me, Mother. It got a little stuffy so I came out for a minute to get some fresh air, and then I heard some noise outside the gate and wanted to see what it was."

The Mother Superior shines her flashlight in my face, and examining me mistrustfully then directs the beam of light towards the gate.

"There are cats out, roaming around."

"Yet the man who was standing here just a moment ago looked nothing like a cat. That was your Leon. Was it not?"

"Leon?" I repeat after her, the name of that stranger unexpectedly becoming as close to me as though I'd known him half my life.

"You know exactly whom I refer to. Don't play the fool with me. Zyta saw you two kissing at the gate once. You must stop these rendezvous, for your own good! The war is hardly the best time for such tomfoolery."

"But, Mother . . ."

"I'm begging you, Anula: do not risk it! I know it's him you've been distributing those papers for."

I try to think of something to say, but at that moment thunder booms. Clouds convulse and scatter out across the sky. The Mother Superior raises her hands and tries to out-shout the storm:

"Margot, you bitch!"

Remembering the newspaper clipping I found on her desk not long ago, I assume she must have known Margot. I can't move. We stand facing one another: me barefoot, shivering in my disheveled pajama, she in a halo of light, her hands raised like a prisoner at roll call.

Fat drops of rain knock loose the rose petals in the fading flowerbeds and hit the dirty concrete.

Over the courtyard hovers the scent of wet dust, so unlike the scent of anything else at all. My morning Latin practice is as prolonged as a Rorate Mass. The instructor scrawls out the third conjugation on the chalkboard:

"*Vivo*, I live, *vivis*, you live, *vivit*, he lives, *vivimus*, we live," she recites. I'm staring out the window.

In the hedge outside the registrar's on Home Army Avenue a magpie ransacks the trash, screeching: *Rorate caeli desuper*, Release the heavens' dew. Then it flies down onto the sidewalk and tries to peck out the eye of a plastic doll lying near the dumpster.

I grind down the words in my mouth, break them down into prime factors in my notebook. I can't wait for my rendezvous with Kamil and try to picture his face, his hands, his lips. But it's hard for me to recreate his image from memory because it still seems so unlike him.

After my classes I flit to the restroom, where I put on mascara, change into a tight bodysuit, switch from my comfortable sneakers into brown wedges. I let down my hair and spritz it with purple Impuls, which smells like cheap knockoff Chanel No. 5, and in a cloud of melted wax, orange, and violets I rush to Staszic Park.

Kamil is waiting for me at the southern end of the park, by the fountain, as promised, and he keeps glancing at his watch. I stop near the weeping willow, where he won't notice me. Perhaps after all these months, from the time of our last meeting in Hektary, I want to take in the sight of him, memorize him once and for all: against the backdrop of the fountain, those sprays sending iridescent Easter bunnies hopping all across his face. Tall, swarthy, with that wavy hair that goes down to his shoulders, he is a Nazarene vision in a stained glass window.

I can't take it anymore and call out his name. He comes up—actually running toward me—and hands me a bouquet of cornflowers and tries to kiss my hand. I'm not into that old-fashioned gesture, which I associate with drooling uncles from harvest fairs, weddings, and name days, and I twist my hand away in self-defense. His lips brush my wrist. This is too much for me. I get up on my tiptoes because even in wedges I'm not that tall, and I want to return his kiss on his just-shaved cheek with its little nicks. I manage to plant my lips on his neck. Kamil puts his arms around me, and then we're both leaning over.

"Let me go!" I squeal in delight.

We take a walk down the Avenue, which was modeled on the boulevards of Paris by a Polish engineer of German descent named Jan Bernhard. After our fifteen-minute promenade around town, we pause at the outbuilding at number 52, where on the façade, above the window of the second story, there is a bust of Johannes Gutenberg.

"There was once a printer's in this building, where Franciszek Wilkoszewski used to publish his National Democracy daily *The Dispatch* and watercolor series with views of the city. I read that he used the type from linotypes in a rotary printing press, but perhaps I'd better quit boring you now. How about we head to Cepelianka for a beer."

Instead of answering, I just take another look around the courtyard, where for some reason, I can hear the rhythmic echoes of the printing presses, the buzz of the typesetting department, the clatter of that linotype.

The setting sun catches our eyes as it shifts slowly into the windows of the annex.

At Cepelianka we sit down by the little pond out back and order two steins of beer. The tipsy bartender disappears around the counter, going back to focusing on his efforts on his Gameboy.

"My God, I'm really worried about you. Why would you want to live in that nunnery? Did they not give you university accommodations?"

"I'm just renting a room with the nuns for now, planning to move out soon," I say, not particularly certain of my own words.

Kamil scoots over towards me and cups my disheveled curls in his hand, sweeps them behind my ear. At his touch my hair becomes electric. These summoned sparks burn like meteorites, then vanish into thin, warm air.

He says, "So I hear there's one professor students call the Brückner of Częstochowa."

"Brankowski?"

"Yes, that's it, Brankowski. He's the one who gets up on top of a bench and gets in lotus pose? He was a monk, right? Or he calls himself a theologian."

"Exactly, that's him. Have you come across him?"

Kamil orders us each another beer and as a carp smacks its lips in the pond he leans forward in his chair and taps the surface of the water with his fingertips. I recognize this gesture and feel my stomach tighten. Instinctually I reach out towards him but withdraw my hand when out of the corner of my eye I see the door to Cepelianka open and then see Piotrek, who goes and stands at the bar, watching us through the window. I move over a little towards the palm, wanting to hide behind it.

"Once Brankowski started talking to me in this academic bookstore," says Kamil, returning to the subject at hand without having noticed a thing, "and he asked to bum a cigarette because, he explained, bacteria won't attack the organism of a smoker. I told him that some organisms are safe regardless, due to just being so closely related."

My exuberant laughter releases the bartender from his enslavement; he sets down his Gameboy and glances around the back patio with his bloodshot eyes. Piotrek finishes his beer, turns on his heel, and stalks out of Cepelianka.

"Is he really hard on you, grade-wise?"

"Who?"

"Dictionary Guy."

"Last Friday he tried to talk a couple of the girls from our cohort into heading up into the Sokole Góry with him, on some sort of excursion."

"What for?"

"I don't think you want to know the kinds of things he gets up to on those excursions. I mean, I've heard he takes the girls on piggyback rides, teaches them to pee standing up, and checks the size of their bra cups."

"What a pig! Does he bother you like that, too?"

"I'm not his type. He likes curvy girls with dark hair. But he has given me some pretty disgusting things to read."

"You should get together and file a complaint with the dean. In Katowice there was a professor like that who told his female students to do a word-formation analysis of the word 'dick.' One of the female lecturers filed a complaint with the university, and after a disciplinary hearing the guy had to go on early retirement."

He talks a moment longer, but I'm no longer listening, contemplating instead the outline of his lips, his skin, his eyes that look like amber under the patio lights. Then he, too, falls silent, tugging at a strip of napkin. We sit staring at each other, relishing the silence, our knees meeting underneath the table.

When by eight Cepelianka gets crowded, we decide to move on to some other, more intimate place. We walk down Second Avenue. All the nooks that have been so important to me since 1994 have suddenly become invisible. Częstochowa sliced through by the tram line: wagons chugging along from the turning loop at Raków on past the North neighborhood slowly accustom me to their rhythm. I don't look as closely at the displays, don't peruse the windows of the classic tenement houses, don't stare stubbornly in at the gates.

I walk intent upon the rhythm of our steps, watching our shadows as they shamelessly slide into one another on the sidewalks.

IN THE ANTIQUITIES CAFÉ, a coffee shop located on the ground floor of a tall building just past the Freedom Cinema, it's empty and cozy. I relax into my armchair, inhaling the fragrance of strong tea. The walls are decorated with male nudes in gilded frames. Atop the round oak tables, candlesticks bulge with wax. Frank Sinatra's soothing elegance transports us back to the times of swinging love affairs. Behind the bar appears a man around fifty with salt-and-pepper hair wearing a suit jacket and a snow-white button-down shirt. We order a pot of Earl Gray to share, little toasts, then beer.

A little tipsy now, Kamil takes me by the hand. "I remember the day I first saw you," he whispers, leaning into me. "I remember it like it was yesterday. It was Sunday. The very start of summer. I was sitting at a little table in your grandfather's room, writing down in my lap the songs he reluctantly dictated—I suspect only because I'd bring him candy and those little bottles of vodka in exchange. I never really felt at home at your place. It wasn't just that everybody in your family seemed so stiff to me, and melancholy, and marked by all these traumas—on top of that, hanging everywhere were taxidermied birds. So one day I went out to smoke in the yard—on the square, as you guys call it—and then as I was going back through the entryway to his room you just landed right on top of me, coming down the ladder from the attic. Your cheek smeared with green paint, smelling of hay and turpentine, you brought into the house with you the light of a summer's day. I think you must have been embarrassed, because you ran out in front of the house and put a bucket on a stump next to the barn and squatted down spreading your legs like a boy to wash your face off. Your underwear was showing. The bucket tipped. Cold water spilled over your bruised knees and bare calves. I wanted to go up to you and say hi and talk, but you didn't even look back at me. You marched off into the fields like you couldn't have cared less."

Nearing eleven we get ready to leave. As he stands, Kamil bumps into a brass ashtray that slides off the table and onto the floor. Both of us bend down for it. I can feel his breath on my forehead, my eyelids, my temples. Our lips meet in the darkness.

THE LAST DAY OF SUMMER is misty and smells like fermented blackberry juice, and it sticks to me and makes me gag. I sit in my room in the attic and try to read what I've been assigned. Briefly I wonder whether the non-believing daughter of a Catholic woman and a Volunteer Reserve Militiaman might still be able to join the oblates and spend a few year living in the Congregation of the Sisters in Christ's Heart, like Sister Anna or Sister Łucja, in the world of old women, where all things are determined by Mother Stanisława and Sister Zyta, where reality intermingles with dreams, present with past, sacred with profane and the mundane with the supernatural, asceticism with eroticism, sin with saintliness; I could really learn Latin, *habita tecum*, delve into the mysteries of my own heart, and write, and read big books as soon as the Mother Superior gets me those entry cards she promised me for the Old Library and the one in Jasna Góra.

I get dizzy; still, I go downstairs.

After lunch I look out the window of the refectory onto the courtyard, where a group of German pilgrims is filing out of the visitors' wing of the congregation, one by one. They stand in a circle, count off and then tuck into small black rucksacks the pins and pennants they purchased at the stalls on Saint Barbara Street and hobble unhurriedly to their bus, which sparkles with the advertising of the transport company Exodus Bremen. When they have all disappeared inside it, Mother Stanisława runs out into the courtyard and spits onto the sidewalk again and again. One of the boys now inside the bus notices her, and evidently recognizing in her the nice old lady who just yesterday had offered him candy in the common room after lunch, now follows her gestures with his nose pressed to the window as she raises her fist against the world.

"She's clearly deteriorated," says Sister Anna, coming into the refectory and standing next to me.

When the bus drives off, the Mother Superior, going back and forth between sobbing and cursing, sits down on a patch of grass. Then Sister Zyta runs up and tries to pick her up, but she can't manage by herself. Soon more sisters join in, forming a row like the line for the turnip the grandfather planted in the garden in Tuwim's poem, all trying to raise up the Mother Superior from the ground.

"Are Sister Zyta and Mother Stanisława siblings?" I ask Sister Anna.

"I never thought about them being related, I always just assumed it was the intimacy of living in close quarters for a long time—but now that you ask, I wonder. The Mother Superior is fairly full-figured, while Sister Zyta is skinny, but there is something alike in their appearances. They have similar movements, and they have the same pageboy haircuts, and they both like to wear black. Although Zyta has more energy, wouldn't you say? I'm sure it hasn't escaped your attention that they run this place together?" Sister Anna shakes the tassel loose and lets down the curtain. "You don't have to worry too much about their commands, you know. They're perfectionists. Have you ever noticed how much time Sister Zyta spends on polishing the Mother Superior's shoes?"

"We do not have mice here," interrupts the Mother Superior, who suddenly appears in the doorway of the refectory, dirty, without her clogs, leaves tangled up in her hair. Seating herself at the table, several meters long, where the oblates consume their three meals daily, she grabs up some breadcrumbs from the wicker basket and stuffs them into her apron pocket with a face that suggests she's afraid someone will take them away from her. "When we got back to our barrack after the roll call we had one under the cot," she sighs. "Remember, Anula?" she turns to me. "You tamed her and kept her in the straw of the mattress and fed her bread crumbs, but that damned Aufseherin Margot finally spotted her and crushed her to death with her truncheon."

At these words I get pale and come close to fainting. I dig my nails into the gritty sill. Sister Anna notices and pulls me away from the window.

"I'm stealing our student away into the garden, Mother," she says to the Mother Superior, who, instead of responding, shuffles barefoot over to the corner of the refectory, where she takes from the newspaper basket a few issues of *Sunday* and wraps up her crumbs in them.

We rush out of the refectory. Sister Anna picks up a bag of dried-out weeds lying in front of the greenhouse and takes me into the boiler room, where she opens slightly the little door to the furnace and in one nervous movement throws the white goosefoot and thistle branches onto the fire. The bitter aroma of the herbs fills the room, startling the moths out of the pipes. The flames devour the little yellowish and lilac flowers.

"I always burn them in here so they won't spread."

She blows from my cheek an uninvited fleck of ash and looks at me with a penetrating gaze, as though wanting to bless me. In alarm I take a step backwards and stumble onto a mousetrap with my clog. The spring clanks. The trap snaps. The wire latch pins down the corner of my skirt. Sister Anna bends down and carefully opens the trap back up.

"Wioletta, you have to move out as fast as you can. You have to," she whispers. "It's what will be best for you, okay? You have to believe me. You never know what the Mother Superior is going to get in her head next."

"Next?" I ask, alarmed.

"Sometimes, to Sister Zyta's great dismay, she brings some student into the congregation, taking her for her daughter who was murdered in the camp."

"I'm not afraid of her."

"I saw that today, how you don't fear her. You try to play the role of Anula especially for the Mother Superior, Wioletta, you're always going to the reading room and looking through the magazines in the archives so you can really get into that world, but it takes its toll on you emotionally. That's not going to turn out well for you at all, okay? You need to get your things in order and escape, okay? Don't drink those herbs the Mother Superior brews for you every day. Do you understand?"

"But . . ."

"You almost fainted today in the refectory. Listen carefully to what I'm about to say. About two years ago your room was occupied by Zuzanna from Poraj. The Mother Superior also made her drink the same herbal concoctions."

"What happened to her?"

"We took her away in the night."

"Took her where?"

"The hospital in Tysiąclecie."

"Jesus!"

"Do you have someplace to go?"

"Not really."

"Family, friends?"

"There is a person, a man, older than me, but he isn't really living in Częstochowa on a full-time basis . . ." I clear my throat.

"My cousin works at the boarding house for Słowacki High School, on Kościuszko Avenue. Her name is Małgorzata. As soon as you're ready, pack your things, go to her and use my name. I don't think there will be any problem with you staying there for a couple of weeks. And here are the keys to the congregation. I made copies yesterday, just in case. The bigger one opens the gate, and the smaller ones open the entrance," she says and slams the furnace shut. Darkness pulsates in the boiler room and under our eyelids.

THE BUS TICKETS GO UP on the first of October. I don't buy the monthly pass, and almost every day I walk back to my accommodations with the sisters, though without the same enthusiasm I had at first. "Every day takes just a little more from me," I jot down in my diary, and I really do get thinner quick, and paler, and have frequent dizzy spells.

At eleven o'clock Piotrek calls at reception and invites me out to the last showing at the movie theater. We meet at three on the Kwadraty, in front of the Megamart, and after eating pierogi ruskie at U Matuli, which is filled with college students, visitors and half the over-sixty population of Częstochowa, we roam around the city plucking the seeds from a sunflower head.

Fall, doled out by the Energetyka clock, pierces with copper and gold the dirty blue between the tenement houses and lends the city softness. Posters of Goplana sitting on a Honda bike from Adam Hanuszkiewicz's *Balladyna* dampen on the poles in front of the center for the promotion of culture, but Piotrek insists we go over onto Freedom to see *Batman*. When we leave the theater, Second Avenue has been taken over by a band of skinheads, thirty-strong, shouting Roman Dmowski slogans. We stand on the corner staring at this procession, our faces looking like we've been transported from Jasna Góra to Gotham City. Piotrek takes my hand and offers to escort me back to the convent, all the way. I say no. Night shrouds us in Bakelite, rolls up the Avenues. The lights of the banks, the pharmacies, the displays of the stores smolder in fog. We stop at the wooden gazebo at Staszic Park to have a little wine.

"You still running around with that old hippie?"

"That's none of your business."

"So he's your man now, huh?"

"Come on."

"Are we still playing this game? Or are you just pretending, to get your revenge?"

"Revenge? I don't know what you're talking about. Maybe you'd better go home."

"You'd better go home, you'd better go home," he mocks me. "Look at the little mommy." He sits down beside me on the bench and rubs my back. "Sorry, I guess I'm a little irritable today."

"A little?"

"Look at me, Wiola." He takes my chin in his hand. "Have I really changed that much in the last few years?"

"What are you talking about?"

"After I moved from Myszków to Częstochowa I bulked up a little, started shaving my head, but I was sure you knew from the start who I was and that you were just kidding around, or else pretending."

He passes me the wine. I drink straight from the bottle.

"From Myszków?"

"You really didn't recognize me that first day at the registrar's?" he asks in the calmest voice. "Then I'll remind you."

He wraps his arms around my waist and kisses me in such a way that I finally lose all control over myself. We lie down on the floor of the gazebo that smells of rotting bark. The larch needles sprinkled around poke into my back and thighs. I feel his cool touch under my denim skirt. Piotrek tears my tights off, putting his hand under my underwear, and although his touch is painful, maladroit, and far too impatient, I want it, I want him, I want.

"I don't want to!" I cry and as I try to scramble up, I scrape my left palm across the rough surface of the floorboard. And a wound long since healed now makes itself known again. Displaced time gets found. Not a minute goes by before I have recalled every last detail.

I'm sixteen years old. The mobile soda fountains rasp around the village's small squares. It's a sunny day. I sit by some buckets on the little main square feverishly measuring out a half-liter container of fruit; the almondy acidic aftertaste of cherry still sits in my mouth. Beside me bustles my grandmother dressed in some five flowery skirts. On my palm, where I got a dirty splinter while picking cherries the day before, a blue streak has appeared. Suddenly Piotr, the boy I'd been going out with for a few weeks and with whom I had fallen in love, comes around the corner, accompanied by his elegant mother, a doctor. I wave to him, but he doesn't return my greeting, just casts an indifferent gaze on me as though I am a stranger.

"That was you!" I say now. "Back then you just . . ."

Piotrek seizes the hem of my skirt, but I pull away from him in time, and with all the strength I have in my legs I run towards Saint Barbara Street.

At the congregation's gate I take off my torn stockings, shake out the larch tree needles from my skirt, try to fix my hair, and with the copied key I received from Sister Anna, I enter into the convent. I pass the dozing porter, grab my clogs from where they're hidden behind the plaster figure of Saint Barbara and go up to the attic, where, exhausted, I fall asleep almost immediately.

At midnight the moon breaks free from a dark blue cloud, slides through the skylight into my room and sways under the ceiling like a helium balloon from which someone is slowly releasing the contents. When the November rain drums against the skylight, I take from my suitcase all the obituaries I always carry with me and set them out on the bed. Obituaries, the dead's full-page IDs, which once in the form of a postcard invited the living to obsequies on behalf of the departed soul. Instead of a PESEL, corners pierced by thumbtacks, vanitas motifs: a skull, rotten or withered fruit, a clock, musical instruments, crosses leaning over under ribbons or palm leaves, the official designation with the letters RIP, the bars above and underneath the I present or absent, wreaths of ivy, pine, juniper, past adverbial participles beleaguered by the wind and rain, sentences in Times New Roman on the transport of the dead.

In the obituaries printed by missionary priests that I recently Xeroxed from Zygmunt Gloger's encyclopedia, the corpse's head is resting on its shins, festoons between the teeth; it's framed by the figure of a snake with a cross made of a scythe and a shovel, and out from the eye sockets poke four ears of wheat. An angel with the face of Larry Flynt slumps against a sarcophagus.

My mom can't stand my funereal hobby, which has obsessed me since high school, or to be more precise, since the time after my cousin's wedding when I ceased to be a phillumenist and lost all desire to keep collecting matchbox labels.

"Have you completely lost your mind? Now it's obituaries? But you'll bring down a curse on our whole family!" she says, and as usual her words go in one ear and right out the other, and with the same zeal with which she burns them in the furnace, I keep bringing home new obituaries and hiding them in the detachable, specially hollowed out table leg where my grandpa once kept his souvenirs from real and imagined enemies: notes on the fates of the stoves he's installed, information on the debtors who owed him for their stone, his button with the eagle in the crown, his army ID, and his Kennkarte.

In late October, when my mother, standing before the yawning proprietor of a funeral home, hesitates as to the design of her mother's—my grandmother's—death notice, I step in and suggest the one with the windmills and shells. In this way, in the waning days of the twentieth century, I link the stories of all the women in my family. Windmills, because their days were dictated by chaff-cutter and mill; shells, because they lived and died in the Jurassic Highland, where beneath the surface roared the sea, imprisoned in dolostone, limestone, marlstone.

"Stefania Lubas, née Walo, died the eighteenth of October, nineteen hundred and ninety-four, having survived seventy-nine years," I read aloud, relishing the past participle clause "having survived."

Stefcia was born in a hut by the forest at the start of the twentieth century, in a world completely dominated by men, and from earliest childhood she grew accustomed to domestic service and to farm chores, until at the age of sixteen she was given in marriage to a man she did not know, one Władek, from Brudzowice. A woman who falls asleep at the kneading board, over the suds-filled wash tub, who faints during her period in the hayloft at the chaff cutter, in the pigsty in pig shit, who goes out behind the barn and buries the placenta and the remains of the babies she loses near the nettles after vinegar rinses and tansy infusions, launders in secret in the well or the stream the linen scraps that serve her as sanitary napkins, mends her husband's and sons' underpants, mending herself and her life by night. Will that girl be able to grow up into a strong, self-aware woman? If after giving birth to or losing six children she survives a few more decades, then maybe she will begin to get the occasional glimpse of who she is. For me, she is a symbol of twentieth-century womanhood, a person who had to play many different roles in her life, in order to keep going. Before she could become a beautiful enchantress, she began to be destroyed by hypothyroidism. I was able to get to know her during that period of transformation, and I observed her disappearing body, went with her to the forest, to the meadows by the quarries to gather herbs, and I sat down with her among the tracts of rye where she would hide her illegal poppy beds. As we traveled over fields she would tell me about the souls of unborn children that lived in the willows' trunks, and she'd sing me ballads as I combed and cut the gray hair she was losing, then gathering it up in bands off the linoleum and throwing it into the stove.

She told me how one night "right around the middle of the war" she heard up on the hill a ruckus of armored cars. She got really scared that time. Władek still hadn't gotten back from the Stalag, and now she had to look out for the children by herself, as well as taking care of the farm and managing anything else that might come up. Now she told the children to hide in the root cellar and sit there and not make any noise. She looked out the window. A blinding light flooded the kitchen. She squinted. She heard enemy conversations in German in the hallway, an offensive of army boots on the hardwood floor. With all her strength she tried to keep from fainting.

An exhausted officer crossed the threshold of the room, sat down in a chair, pointed with his polished boot and his Mauser to some fresh bread covered in a starched cloth. She understood. She ran up to the table, laid the loaf on her breast as her mother had taught her, cut it in thick slices and spread butter over each. Never in her life had her hands shaken the way they did then. The German slid off his glasses, wiped them on his sleeve, and gave her a long, hard look. Slowly he ate the bread, still watching her. The clock ticked. Shadows glided across the floor. The dog thrashed on his chain by the shed. Suddenly the officer stood and began to wander around the room, peering into the clay jug where the rye meal was souring. He went up to her and whispered something in German. Then he called his subordinates, gave some orders, and nodding farewell, quickly left the kitchen.

To her surprise, the Germans only took a sack of flour and three ducks from the coop, and then they left. Twenty minutes later, she went to see the children, wanting to make sure they were okay. She told them to spend the night in the barn, just in case. She herself lay down on the floor by the brooder and sobbed all night long. Only around dawn did her fear let go, and then she was able to breathe a sigh of relief.

She remembered the German officer's short utterance, as though sensing that those foreign, hastily spoken words had some connection with the fact her life got spared. Just after the liberation she rode her bicycle to the local library and requested a dictionary. With the help of the librarian, who knew a little German, she translated the officer's words, which came from Goethe's *Faust*: "The eternal feminine draws us on high."

"Traveling? What do you want that for? You'll wander aimless like your father," she would say whenever I asked her to lend me a little money so I could go somewhere. A woman who gave birth to five children at home on a straw mattress, never crossed the border of the Katowice province, walked the same paths for seventy years, yet knew the world better than any number of self-proclaimed Herodotuses. She would stand in the yard, put the base of her hand up to her forehead and gaze out at the horizon, instantly understanding when floods or storms or plagues of potato bugs would come or that some stranger was wandering in the night among the blackthorn bushes up on the hill. Trips filled her with fear because those of her nearest and dearest who left the village lost their lives, like her daughter, Anna, or came back only half-alive and broken, like her husband from the Stalag. And yet she always asked to be told about the Errant Rocks in the Central Sudetes, the Skull Chapel in Czermna, the mechanical nativity scene in Wambierzyce, the taste of the grapes from the Žilina region.

We would often go out into the fields together. She would gather herbs, while I would lie down on that ground covered in chicory and cheddar pinks, feather grass, Michaelmas-daisies, steppe cherries, mountain liveforevers and stemless carline thistles, staring into the sun. Past the horizon, the ocean swelled.

1996, THE NEW YEAR, has snuck up on me. The melodic voice of the radio host informs listeners of wounded Brits in Sarajevo, quintuplets in Opole, the upcoming finale of the Great Orchestra of Christmas Charity. In his New Year's address, the new president, Aleksander Kwaśniewski, proclaims the adoption of a new constitution the most pressing challenge of the coming year. Due to the flu epidemic, the Ministry of Health asks superintendents and local officials to extend holiday breaks.

Due to the hike in electricity and gas, the Mother Superior now has us turn off all the lights in the dormitories at nine o'clock at night. Until nine, I slide up and down the corridor, buffing the floor, feeling like newly appointed figure skating champion Chen Lu, my braid tied with a black bow. Suddenly the doors to the corridor open to reveal the Mother Superior. I have too much momentum to brake in time and skate straight into her. We fall in a heap together onto the gleaming floor. A moment later, the Mother Superior stands, brushes off her pleated skirt, and instead of chastening me as usual for my bad behavior, my clowning around, my wild swoops around objects of religious significance, she invites me into her room for tea.

I wipe my wet hands on the apron I've hung over the railing of the stairs and follow the Mother Superior to the second floor of the southern wing. She heats some water in an electric kettle, then brews the tea. We sit in silence for a long while, during which time she watches me very carefully, as though wanting to paint my portrait. A nun moth turns on a knot in an oak shelf and travels up the wall towards a table lamp that's switched on.

"Have you seen how many Germans have been roving around?" Stanisława begins at last, in a hushed croak.

I finish my tea, which tastes bitter, like wormwood, and I agree with her, thinking she has in mind the frequent pilgrims who come from Germany.

I play with the deer-patterned wool blanket that covers my armchair and, yawning, I look over at the volumes displayed on the oak bookcase.

"Remember how they dragged him out of the apartment in September?"

"Who?"

"Your father."

"I think so," I say reluctantly, having been instructed that during flare-ups of the Mother Superior's illness the best response is silence or agreement.

"I didn't tell you, but I sent you to Aunt Zyta then, and I went with that Wehrmacht officer who was a Silesian and spoke good Polish. Remember?"

"I . . ."

"I let it happen, and then I begged him to—I don't know what. The Germans were already herding them over to the gathering point on Mirowska. They searched them there and marched them out again, to the jail over in Zawodzie, but the jail was so full already they couldn't fit another soul. I ran down Warszawska between burning buildings to Cathedral Square! I saw them, your father and your uncle. They were all standing there. After about ten minutes Bishop Wróblewski came, the Germans had summoned him, and he opened up the cathedral. I hid at the gate. My heart was pounding. I saw the thrilled faces of those Germans, and I just knew they'd open fire. And the machine guns started rattling, and that was the end. Oh God, they didn't make into the cathedral . . ."

I turn towards the window, where the wind is tearing at the branches of the pine tree and knocking yellowed needles onto the sill. That wind again, I think, remembering the night I first met Mother Stanisława on New Year's Eve at the train station. Anxiously I set my teacup down on the little table and make as if to leave. The Mother Superior stands up, too, and blocks my path, knocking over the lamp, which scatters streaks of light from the floor up along the pale walls, transforming the room into the cabin of a ship on choppy waters. Then she stuns me by kneeling beside the bed and pulling out from under it a dusty trunk.

"Pack your things, Anula!" she orders me. "You have to get out of here as fast as you can! They'll be here any minute!" She opens drawers and throws their contents onto the floor: slips, kerchiefs, a pilled serdak, silk stockings riddled with runs, Ultrasol cream, Elida soap, a wooden brush with gray hairs in it. And instead of holding her back or arguing with her or even just running out of the room, I help her pack the things into the trunk. After letting her confuse me with her daughter who was sent to the gas chamber by Margot Kunz at Ravensbrück, I feel it's too late now. Our fates have been intertwined since the night we met at the station, and in some sense, I have become Anula: I respond to her name, I do my hair as she did, with the part in the middle, I wear her gold cameo ring, I dress in her skirt and blouse, and every day I absorb more of the smell of those clothes. Yes, I want to be Anula, have dresses tailor-made for me at Foltyński's, put on patent leather shoes and silk stockings and sip tea out of a porcelain cup come evening, read *The Częstochowa Dispatch* and *Illustrated Weekly*, attend my classes at the Juliusz Słowacki School for Girls, dress up as Queen Jadwiga or an elf to take part in the carnival parade down the Avenues with my mother and father and uncle and Aunt Zyta, see *The Rage of Paris* with Danielle Darrieux at the Luna Theater, secretly go to a palm reader who lives in a trailer opposite the fire brigade and hear how based on a broken life line, knots in my heart line and changes of direction in my fate line she predicts a passionate love for an older man, tells me tales of a long life and overseas travels; I want to go on excursions to glassworks like Anula, go to Krynica, Rabka, to the rocks just over at Olsztyn, to the Zofia Villa that belongs to the administrators of my school and that sits at the base of the ruins of the Olsztyn Castle, near the road; I want to be shown around Abraham's on Nadrzeczna and try on all the most fashionable hats, to go for tea at the Grand Café, to be a pampered young lady from a good home and in the trolley on the way to the Wieluński Market to snuggle up to my lavender-scented mother.

"You'll go to Olsztyn now, to Aunt Bronka."

The Mother Superior looks around the room as though searching for a passageway to another era, when announcements from Der Stadthauptmann hung over the walls, and Częstochowa was crossed by Adolf-Hitler-Allee, while the Ration Card Sales Bureau was located at Dąbrowski 11, and the Adolf & Eduard Holler Freight Forwarding Company could ensure a quick and painless customs clearance, as well as storage, insurance, regular transport, and group wagons.

"Do you remember her address?"

"I don't think I do," I answer with a voice that is no longer my own.

"That's all right. I'll put it down on this paper for you . . . or perhaps not, that would be unwise in times like these. You'll have to learn it by heart. Repeat after me . . ."

"Stasia? Stasia, what the hell are you doing to her?" says Zyta in her hoarse voice, from the other side of the door.

"Get out of here!" screams the Mother Superior and runs to the door to close the latch. But Sister Zyta manages to shove her way inside the room.

"You're always interfering. You were supposed to not let me see you with that pharmacist husband of yours. He's the one who denounced Anula. Is that not right?"

"How can you say that? After what he did for you both?

Do you no longer remember how you and I contracted typhoid fever in forty-three? Who was it who took care of Anula then? Who was the one who kept on bringing you your soup? Hunh?"

"Go away!"

"But I'm her godmother, for heaven's sake. And if you must know, it was Sapota who reported her to the Gestapo, not my Stefan," she says artificially, as though reciting an old and long-rehearsed speech.

"Sapota? Wiesiek Sapota? Come on, we were in school together. You told me he was shot over by the railroad tracks." She sits down on her bed and keeps talking, but her words get drowned out by an ambulance approaching. "They're already here. It's too late!"

"We have to get Anula off to Aunt Bronka's in the country right away."

"But how, by God? Father sold the automobile back before the war."

"I hired a wagoner. He's waiting out front. You stay here, and I'll take Anula out."

Time in the room condenses, drips viscous as the candles in the nearby cathedral. Sister Zyta grabs me by the wrist with her bony fingers and drags me toward the door. I wrench myself out of her grasp and go to the Mother Superior and kiss her hand.

"You take care, child." She sniffs, then shudders as though waking up suddenly from a deep sleep and landing in another dimension of time; holding a pillow to her breast, she rocks it, humming, "Oh little star, something glimmered when I glimpsed the world. Why is it, little star, your beam has dimmed?"

I stride obediently after Sister Zyta, first down the stairs, into the vestibule, where in the corner an impeccably packed suitcase awaits me. Sister Zyta pulls harder on her invisible strings, leading me like a marionette out into the courtyard, down the sidewalk along the wall, straight to the iron gate.

"Hand me your keys!"

I reach into my skirt pocket and give her my key clip with the matryoshka on it. "Don't you come around her again, you hear me?" She squeezes a wad of cash into my hand. "It'll be better that way," she adds, not looking me in the eye. "Do you understand? May God be with you, child," she says, a little more gently, with tears in her eyes, and turning on her heel, she hurries away.

I want to run after her, shout, give back the money and above all say goodbye to Sister Anna, whose face flashes in the second-floor window of the dormitory, but the iron gate has already slammed behind me, shutting me out.

3.
Hey, Sleeping Beauty

MY CLOGS CLATTER down the pavement. Rydzyk peeks out from my coat pocket. In front of the train station, which has suddenly grown a turret in the shape of a locomotive, a crowd has gathered, and I hear the clatter of horses' hooves, the melodies of barrel organs, shouts from carriage drivers and paperboys:

"Get your National Lottery tickets at the Antoni Eger Lottery Office, fourteen First Ave!" hollers a boy dressed in a patched-up double-breasted coat. "Regular number of big winners!"

"Unprecedented Czech assault on Polish territory! The battle for Olza rages on. Will England surrender the colonies to Deutschland? Read *The Częstochowa Dispatch*. Just ten groszy!"

I pick up a paper off a bench: October 2, 1938. The Feast of the Guardian Angels. Sunday. Sunrise 5:44 am. Sunset 5:22 pm.

I read that the Dwernicki Walls are to be covered in slag from the railway bridge on. Several electric lamps will be added to the streets so that the darkness that's prevailed thus far does not give rise to "unsavory practices." A moment later I pass a strange procession of local officials marching stiff as mannequins, scarcely shuffling their feet, only pausing so that the shoe-shiners can polish their slippers with their rags. An orchestra of tram conductors accompanies. Red and white pennants flutter on poles with sirens carved upon their tops. They're headed straight for the Cathedral of Our Lady in Jasna Góra. I follow them as though hypnotized and listen as they cheer for President Ignacy Mościcki and Marshal Śmigły-Rydz.

Begging pilgrims sit along the wall with signs around their necks. Next to a covered cart crouches a vendor woman wearing a black kerchief on her head who tries to force a grayish yellow quarter of soap that reeks of tallow and reads *Schicht* into my hand. At the odor of decaying corpses I shudder and run off to the gate.

An hour goes by. Now the walls display announcements from the fourth of November, nineteen thirty-nine:

> *With the establishment of the General Government, following the introduction of military protection of Polish areas under German supervision, the historical episode brought on by the blind government clique of the former Polish nation as well as the hypocritical insurgents in England may now be considered concluded. German army divisions have restored order to the Polish lands. A renewed threat to European peace by means of unjustifiable demands for a state entity that shall never rear its ugly head again . . .*

An hour later, standing at an exhibit of devotional articles, I stare at crucifixes, lamps and carpets. Between

January and February of forty-three suddenly everything is put up for sale—cheap, one-time, instant—light coats, fur coats, broadtail fur coats, silver fox coats, otter collars, grand pianos, stallions, two nickel-plated chandeliers, table lamps and an electric teapot, a pot and a stove, a modern imported piano, a Singer sewing machine, a candy maker and its drum, knee-high boots, a winter coat with a muff for a young girl, a photographic camera, a brown men's hat, a women's mannequin, a child's fur, a cabbage barrel, an infant child, for free, for keeps (male).

I walk through Staszic Park; I pass wooden rows of chairs that bow before the monastery; I stop for a moment at the Lubomirski Gate and then head straight into the cloister, where renovations are underway. Under a low ceiling hangs a yellow sign that says: "Attention! Workers overhead."

"WANNA LOOK WHERE you're going, slut?" At the door to the McDonald's on Freedom Avenue a pimply blond wearing a striped uniform pops up, then tries to pick up the folder I've knocked out of his hands while racing down the sidewalk. But then the blond says, "Wiolka? Wiolka Rogala? It's been ages. Barely recognized you, you've gotten so thin you're just skin and bones now. I think the last time I saw you was that night you left me out to dry at that bus stop by the main road, but I don't hold a grudge, I don't hold grudges . . ."

He glances in surprise at my clogs, which I forgot to take off after Sister Zyta threw me out of the convent, and when Rydzyk peeks out of my coat pocket, he makes a face and takes a slight step back. I want to explain to him, but the sidewalk is still swaying, and then I fall down right onto the folder with the colorful hamburger.

"Elder Lubush?" I mumble. "Did you read the General Government's proclamation? Were you sent here in punishment, as well?"

"What punishment, girl? Sent me where? What are you talking about? I got myself this job." He examines me for a moment. "You've changed, friend . . . I can't believe you, drugged out with a suitcase and a rat, wandering around town? Where'd you get him from? You break into the zoo?"

"Drugged? Me?"

"Oh, come on. It's pretty obvious. What are you even doing here?"

"Majoring in philology."

"In the middle of the night?"

"Oh my god, is it night already?"

"Man, what a major. I'd never have thought you'd become the old Polish schoolmarm."

"Just kind of happened that way I guess."

"You're not looking for work, are you? We need a hostess for the lobby."

"A what?"

"You know, a hostess, like a general waitress," he says in an impatient tone. "The kind that gives out balloons, mops the floor, picks up the cake from the bakery for the clients' birthdays, wipes off the tables and the trays. That's basically what it entails."

"Could I come in just in the evenings?"

"Sure."

"That would be great. Ever since my grandma died, it's been hard to stay afloat in the big city."

"Let's go talk to the boss about it. She's real laid-back. She'll hire you for sure."

Suddenly my body starts to itch as though someone has dropped some turnips down my blouse. My fingertips get numb. Very carefully, I set Rydzyk down on a gleaming tabletop. The lamps along Freedom Avenue are coming undone from their posts; they clatter onto the asphalt and, like billiard balls, roll down the tram tracks.

"Shoot, Lajboś, where're you running off to? You'll be swallowed up by bright dark nebulae. Don't go that way, brother," I mumble, covering my eyes with a hand because the headlights of oncoming traffic are hurting me. "You know, my name is actually Anula. In the gas chamber I went towards the light," I tell him, reciting my own poem. "At the timber yard the scent of resin drifts as I play hide and seek with my mother . . ."

"Aw, man, you're so fucked up," whispers a shaken Lajboś, and just in case, he shuts the door to the restaurant. "Did you just go out because of Saturday? Maybe somebody slipped you something, in your drin, in, in, in . . ."

Snippets of his words seem to make their way to me from some vast distance; the film breaks off.

"ARE YOU THERE?" I hear the voice of Sister Anna, who is standing next to me in the boiler room and passing me dry stalks to burn.

"Here!" I respond emphatically, as if to prove my presence to myself. "I think I've been poisoned, Sister, I feel really weak, I can't stand up anymore."

I need to get some fresh air, I go up to the little window and stand in the glow of the late afternoon sun, letting the light play out across the surface of my face.

"Is she asleep?" says someone. I try to open my eyes, but I can't. My lids are too heavy, maybe glued.

"Yeah, she's asleep. This is that daughter of that Zosia from Hektary. You guys remember the beautiful Zosia, the one half the village was in love with?"

"But the one who loved her the most was Gienek the Combine Driver. Big dumb teddy bear."

"Okay, but what's the girl doing here, with you?"

"Well, she's sleeping, and she's raving about being some Anula. I didn't think she was going to wake up again, to be honest. Jacuś brought her over three days ago in a taxi. She was in a terrible state. Filthy, highly agitated.

"What was wrong with her?"

"I think some hooligans must have drugged her, but to be honest I don't know what happened. When Jacuś found her, she was roving the city by herself."

"My God, such times. You can't even leave your house anymore—we used to walk around on our own all the time, go to carnival."

"Have you ever seen somebody sleep uninterrupted for three days, Józefka?"

"My dad slept like that when he came back from the war, but he really didn't ever wake up again after that."

"Well don't despair. She's young. She'll come out of it."

"You think I should call a doctor?"

"Eh, I don't think you need to. Her cheeks are pretty pink. Let's just give her some milk."

"Good point. Milk detoxifies."

"Did she just move her eyes a little?"

I open my eyes. Above me stand the three Moirai. The first is the seller of the *Schicht* soap from my dream. The second is Jadzia Nowak, Elder Lajboś's aunt, and the third and youngest resembles that snack bar attendant from the train station.

As I stand on the platform for the tram I take daily from Aunt Jadzia's apartment to school, I eavesdrop on my fellow passengers, whose conversations at daybreak are like the slight scrape along the ground of an apple peel. Sleepy, they move their lips, but only their hands really converse; in an odd sequence of gestures they clutch at the air or grasp onto metal, rocking against the railings like tissue paper flowers on their wires. The spring morning is already swollen with light. I look around the tram, where in an instant everything freezes mid-motion, in its smell, in its shape, as though I'd just hit pause. Staring into reflections of faces, deformed in the dirty panes covered in advertisements and announcements, I think about how someday people will learn to bend space-time, travel from space station to space station, from one specular portal to the next.

When after my classes I'm returning to the North district, Professor Brankowski unexpectedly appears at the tram door, takes the empty seat beside me.

"Well, well, who do we have here. Greetings, Sleeping Beauty." He doffs his cap, then falls silent, and like a Janus statue from the island of Boa stares at the other passengers in disgust. Dressed in his usual moth-eaten tweed jacket, white gloves and plastic glasses from a street vendor, he looks like a kind of moth-man heading to a costume party.

"Try these on," he says and slips his specs onto my nose. "With glasses like these you look at the world like a wasp would: they divvy up your view of the world and protect you from dangerous radiation coming from the cosmos."

Amused, I look at his overstuffed plastic bags. The professor shows me their contents: tomatoes with specks of mold, potatoes and withered greens he tells me he gathered out of the trash outside the discount grocery store in Tysiąclecie.

We get off at the Polonia Hall stop. I find myself picking up some of his bags and helping him cart them up to his apartment. We pause on the staircase, where the professor peeks into the little hole in the mailbox.

"I'd like to invite you in for some soup," he says, without taking his eyes off the perforated mailbox with flyers sticking out of it.

Thinking of his antics at school, I hesitate, fearful of going with him into his apartment, yet to my own astonishment, I accept his invitation. For some reason, I am fascinated by his psychopathic nature.

A few minutes later we are sitting in the kitchen, chatting like old friends. The professor heats up yesterday's tomato soup, made out of other vegetable trophies, on the gas stove. The apartment fills with the smell of stewed tomatoes. The soup turns out to be delicious. But the professor doesn't eat, smoking cigarette after cigarette instead, spinning yarns about humanity, which after the flood got divided into Semites and anti-Semites; Troy, which he believes lay on the Adriatic; the Polish language, which is in fact Ukrainian; the Huns, who were all Slavs; the fact that Christianity existed in Poland a century earlier than has been believed; that Siemowit was the great-grandson of Ruryt; and that the Polan tribe bore some relation to the Bavarians.

"There's something in you," he says suddenly, looking me in the eye, "that's elusive somehow. This morning I was planning on walking home, but when the tram came up to the stop, your face in the window flashed by. What were you thinking about in that moment? What were you thinking?"

"Oh, I don't remember, Professor."

"You don't really look, but you do see, right?"

I glance down, and the professor, realizing he's not going to get an answer out of me, waves his hand and walks out into the entryway. I hear him dragging up a stool and then clambering up onto it and having a much harder time than when he showed us the lotus flower in the classroom; then he opens a cupboard and throws something down onto the floor. He returns with a large tube, from which he takes out an old map of the Polish Jurassic Highland. We unroll it on the bench in the big room. The professor sits next to me on the sofa bed and for a long time he just shows me his favorite brooks, groves, and caves, though as evening approaches, he begins to slow down, until finally he lays his gray head somewhere in the Gypsy Rocks on the Eagle's Nest path and falls asleep. He breathes heavily, as though there were some limestone sediment in his lungs. I look at him for a moment. The tension dissolves from his face as it sinks into sleep. His eyelids, covered in a network of maroon veins, vibrate.

In him awakens that boy, touching the wall, the cold forehead of his mother who was shot dead hours ago. When morning comes, he leaves the shelter along with others and runs, like I did once on New Year's, down the path into the fields. It's cold out. His broken boots squelch. The wet bands his mother wrapped his legs in a few days before their flight from the bombarded city have begun to rot. The distance, unknown and rustling with frost, appears infinite and dark. Finally some lights pierce through it. A stone home reminiscent of his ancestral manor appears. He goes up to the gate, where he sees the inscription *Ordo et pax* carved into the wood. He lowers the brass knocker with its coat of arms with the cross.

The professor twitches anxiously, is pale, finally slides down onto the sofa bed. I lean over him and look on in disgust, remembering all his vile behavior, his attacks on female students, his abuse of his power as rector. For a moment I feel like punishing him, tossing his collection of valuable volumes into the garbage chute, pouring tomato soup all over his favorite maps, but I can't bring myself to do it. Making sure he's breathing, I cover him up with a blanket, turn off the light, and leave his apartment.

ON THE EIGHTH OF APRIL, on Easter Monday, I wake up in Aunt Jadzia's apartment, surprised the skylight has left the ceiling, that I can't watch the shining sky in my first waking moments. It's still hard for me to believe that I don't have to leap out of bed before daybreak and make my bed perfectly and check at the door for Mother Stanisława's instructions. Instead, having slept my fill, I sit back down on the duvet, stretch out, and out of habit look around for my clogs.

After breakfast, Aunt Jadzia goes to church, absent-mindedly leaving the door ajar. The aroma of the cheap perfumes the neighbors spray each other with in honor of Dyngus Day wafts in from the building's halls. Gleaming pale green willow branches smack into the windows. Over the North housing development a dark cloud hangs heavy like a slack-baked cake. By the dumpster, just behind the little wall, boys lie in wait for passersby with water toys, buckets, and plastic bottles. Taking advantage of Aunt Jadzia not being at home, I open up my suitcase and take out the wad of bills Sister Zyta pressed upon me back in February, by means of farewell, now hidden in the pages of *Urania*. I count quickly. It's over a thousand zlotys—enough for two months' rent. I rush to gather up my books, my cosmetics, and my notes, which in the course of my mad dash between my job at McDonald's and my classes I've scattered all over the whole room.

An hour later, when my aunt comes back from church and changes into her housedress in the kitchen, I go up to her and hand her a box of chocolates and a pack of coffee.

"Already? You should have warned me."

"I didn't want to upset you in the lead-up to the holidays."

"You could have at least stayed with me until the break."

"I can't." I kiss her on the cheek. "Thank you for everything."

"No trouble at all, my dear. But where are you going to go now? Don't tell me you're going back to those nuns who were poisoning you." She gives me a worried look.

"No, no, I've rented a studio apartment on Lelewel. I'll be closer to work and just in general," I say in an uncertain tone, and I swallow because I'm aware that the real reason for my moving out is something else. I've long dreamed of having my own place, where I can meet with Kamil.

"Do you want something to eat before you go?"

"No thanks, I'm not hungry."

"Have you packed up all your things already?"

"I think so."

"Wait a second. Lest I forget. I've wanted to give you this for a long time now," says Aunt Jadzia and reaches into the pocket of her housedress and hands me a crumpled photograph. "They came to visit once upon a time, your mom and Ania," she says, as she accompanies me to the door.

I drag my suitcase toward the tram terminal. When I get there, I take the picture out of my purse and take a good look at it. Two very young blondes are sitting on a bench in Staszic Park. It's early spring, just like it is now. The chestnuts are in bloom. Aunt Ania looks worldlier, fashionable in her poppy-patterned dress with bell sleeves and wedge heels, looking provocatively from under painted lashes, straight into the lens. My mother isn't wearing any makeup; in a V-neck sweater and a pleated skirt, she clasps her beat-up purse. It must have been her first time in the city, I think, as suddenly a merry cackle bursts from behind the kiosk. A group of teenaged boys runs up to me. I am drenched in bucketfuls of ice-cold water.

Around eleven, towards the end of my shift at McDonald's, Elder Lajboś barges breathlessly into the employees' area.

"Remember that night when those nuns OD'ed you and kicked you out of their convent?" he says to me.

"Let's just say it rings a bell, Lajboś."

"I took you to Aunt Jadzia's place in a taxi and then I got you a job in the lobby."

I shrug.

"And despite the fact you just left me at that bus stop that time I never made you feel bad."

I shrug again.

"Well now I've got a favor to ask."

"Continue."

"Would you be willing to keep this chick at your spot for a couple of days?"

"You mean a girlfriend of yours?"

"Sure. It's just a tough time because she's been sleeping out back here on some cardboard ever since her mom kicked her out of the house."

"How old is she?"

"Eighteen."

"Do I look like an idiot?"

"Okay, okay. Sorry. Sixteen."

"Why can't she stay at your place?"

"Are you nuts? Don't you remember my folks?"

I have no intention of hiding some underage girl in my rented apartment, but when one evening a girl in tears and soaked to the bone knocks on my door, I can hardly turn her away. Kasia, as it turns out she's called, quickly makes herself at home: during the day, she is either sleeping or vomiting, and in the evenings, after availing herself of the contents of my fridge, my bathroom cabinet, and my coin purse, she heads out to the Vacance nightclub. Elder Lajboś visits her rarely, but every few days Kasia does receive her forty-year-old uncle, who is a vicar in one of the parishes around Częstochowa. The priest's frequent visits do not strike me as strange, since I have a clergyman in my family too—my grandpa's cousin, a respected rector—so I don't give too much thought to what goes on in my apartment when I'm not there.

One Saturday, however, I'm not feeling well and decide to leave work a little early. I turn the key in the door, then stand frozen in the entryway. Kasia, wrapped in a towel, is sitting on the mattress, resting her legs on a stool. Beside her, on the floor, kneels the half-naked vicar, splattered with cream, in the middle of shaving the girl's right calf.

"I'm—I'm—I'm sorry," I stutter, and stumbling over the articles of clothing lying on the floor, I step into the kitchen, where through a crack in the door I secretly watch as Kasia and her uncle pack up as fast as they can and run out of my apartment. In the late morning I stop by the registrar's, where I receive the news of a dorm room allotment with indifference. After I get back to my apartment I read over my notes for my classes and write a paper on Stefan Grabiński, a Galician writer who suffered from tuberculosis, woke up in the middle of the night, wandered down train station halls, fell asleep on benches, made quick visits to the old railway casino, chatted with conductors, and in feverish states wrote anecdotes of railwaymen and horror stories made up of ghost trains, hallucinations, a lost station, a blind track where passengers would disappear like in the Bermuda Triangle and the phantasmagoric giant of Smoluch, who appeared on trains and called forth railway calamities. I read and think about the Częstochowa train station, where I met Mother Stanisława, where Scurvy told me about Clod, where Waldek awaits his Adelka. As Grabiński writes, the exuberant life of train stations gets placed in too tight a frame, and so it rhythmically overflows. The chaotic buzz of passengers, the calls of porters, the shrill calls of whistles, the roar of escaping steam all combine into a vertiginous symphony that causes you to lose yourself, gives back a smaller, dazed version of your ego on a wave of some potent element that can carry, rock, intoxicate. In the end, on account of his advanced tuberculosis, he retreated from life, settled in Brzuchowice, a spa outside of what's now called Lviv, where, like Clod from Częstochowa, he spent hours on end walking along train tracks.

Listening to the radio, I fall asleep. At half past five I drag myself off my mattress to take a shower and change into my uniform. I stick the gold hostess badge—on which, unlike my colleagues at work, I have no stars—onto the little pocket of my white blouse, fix my hair in the mandatory braid and go off to work.

The lobby hours are long. Trays fall onto the floor. The helium I inhaled as I inflated the balloons enables me to last until the end of my shift. After taking two laps around the dining area, several strolls on behalf of order pickups outside the restaurant and checking the restrooms three times, finding a cufflink on the vomit-covered sink, I pray the shift manager doesn't call me over for fries. In the end, tired, I bump into the fire alarm with a tray. An evacuation begins. The shift manager runs to the door and opens it wide, asking everyone to calmly leave the dining room and head outside. First mothers with children, then everybody else. I stand paralyzed and squeeze a balloon with the distorted image of Ronald McDonald so hard it bursts with a bang, which heightens the panic in the restaurant considerably. One of the teenagers steals lunch from the next table and tosses it into his bag. A young mother, unable to undo the straps of the highchair where her several-month-old daughter sits, nervously tugs at the child and would no doubt have dislocated his little hands had not a man run up to help her release the clasps.

Completely saturated in frying oil, half-dead and called by the shift manager everything from retard to loser to lubberly cunt, barely able to see out of one eye, my hair sprinkled with salt crystals, I leave work and go and sit out on the Kwadraty by the Megamart. My fingers reek of Domestos.

Salt irritates the burns on my wrists. It's so quiet I can hear the rainwater flowing in streams down the manholes to the sewers. I decide that after I get next month's paycheck I will quit my job in fast food, give up my studio apartment, and either move into the dorm or leave Częstochowa. My days are intertwining dangerously, creating a knot that draws tighter and tighter and tighter: classes-homework-work, classes-homework-work. Between these, the dizzying days of longing for Kamil, who—because of his mother's illness—often goes to Katowice. The demons of desire, as well as an irrational fear of intimacy, transform with time into an explosive mixture. Erotic tension brings on dizziness and stomach pain. He makes me sick. My fingers long for him. I fall asleep thinking about him, as aroused as if I'd spent half my short life in some tantric marathon. His hands are subtle but decisive, his fingers like Paganini's, his lips sensual and full. He a gorgeous and confident Svetovid, I a quiet samo-diva, lost in the metropolis.

In order to calm myself, I decide to stop by Jasna Góra, to watch the pilgrims, breathe the monastery air, and pine away in peace for Kamil and Sister Anna. By the Lubomirski Gate a couple passes me. I turn around and recognize Kasia's face. Behind her, with a baby in a sling, trots a broad-shouldered guy with a shaved head. I realize it's Piotrek.

SOMETIME AFTER ELEVEN I leave work and turn onto a deserted Dwernicki, planning to pass through the little market that way, in front of the twin towers at Lelewel Street. Around the butcher's I hear some noise that resembles soles pounding against asphalt. Unnerved, I speed up. Pale blue lights glow inside the empty meat market. On the wall, beneath the stern face of Our Lady of Częstochowa, portraits of Lech Wałęsa and John Paul II, strings of sausages dangle. I look away. The shadows of two figures emerge from around the corner. Facing me are two skinheads in balaclavas. Dressed in tough jackets with orange lining, they look like demons that have crawled out from some dark cavern in search of a feast.

"Aw, man, it's you, hey, fuck. That's Piotrek's bitch, that asshole from our building who went after you when you tried to fuck with that little cousin of his, you know, that Kaśka."

"Hunh?"

"Man, fuck, take a good look, man. Don't you see who that is? It's that little blonde that was standing out there in front of the movie theater with him that time we fucked up the city last fall."

"You know what, you're right, that is her."

This taller one leaps up to me now, trying to grab me by my left forearm so he can draw me into the corner behind the dumpster, where it stinks of piss and mold; a Nazi song plays on a boom box.

I want to scream, but I can't. My voice dies in my larynx. I duck to avoid the skinhead and run off towards the tracks, coming to a stop before a fence where the philharmonic is. I swallow and, instinctively leaning forward, seize onto the white railing with both hands. The skinhead catches up with me and tries to pull me down. The hooks and eyes on my coat snap apart, their wooden pegs clattering down onto the ground. The pain in my forearm stupefies me for a second. From the direction of the philharmonic train lights pulse, slipping through the fence and settling in a patina over the aspens' leaves. The litter-strewn section of the market is momentarily transformed into a lit circus arena. Just when I finally can't take the pain anymore, and my hands begin to slide off the rail, some jubilant men come out from the direction of the Business Center. Between them steps a well-dressed, dark-haired woman, clacking her heels over the concrete, leaning on the arm of a short, limping man in a cap.

But that's Waldek, I think.

"Natka, *smotree!*" Alex shouts at full volume, and even the skinhead trying to drag me down looks up and towards him.

"*Vot chort!*" Sergey echoes.

Natka, like an experienced lion tamer, gives the signal with her index finger. Instantly the brothers leap into action and are racing towards me. The skinheads let me go and retreat towards the other end of the market. In the corner by the dumpster a fight breaks out; the drunken locals have no chance against two guys brought up on the training grounds of Siberia. I shut my eyes for a second; when I open them, the baldheaded thugs are gone. All that's left of them is some bloodstains, their trampled balaclavas, and the screws, valves and springs of the boom box scattered at the gate.

"*Mudaki!*" Sergey spits on the sidewalk and, with one loafer, crushes the valve of the boom box that has been swaying at his feet.

"*S toboy fsyo f poryadkie?*" Alex asks me, and then comes down from the footbridge. I don't answer, I can't get any words out. I'm still frantically pressing my hands together and relax only when Waldek comes up.

"That's it, college kid, it's over." He pats me on the back. The rose tattooed on his hand flashes before my eyes. For some reason, I have this feeling that the appearance of the Vega people at the Dwernicki Market isn't an accident. I still can't say anything. Natka takes my stiff hands, where a few paint chips still glisten, and applies them to her powdered cheeks.

"You can't just wander around the city like this at night. Fortunately we arrived in time." She pokes a French tip into the tip of my nose.

I want to say something, to say thank you, but I can't manage to get a single word out. I just bow my head and glance at the two cream-colored towers, remember I'm supposed to meet Kamil. Lest the next set of people should arrive, I turn and head quickly towards the apartment buildings.

"Come and visit us sometime at the Vega, college kid!" Waldek shouts after me.

"Stop by whenever you like, and forgive me," Natka adds more quietly.

"*Mudaki*," repeats Sergey, staring at the dark gate, and then he adds something else, but his words are drowned out by the rumble of a passing train.

KAMIL IS WAITING for me in front of the building, leaning on his Fiat.

"Don't tell me: they kept you late at work again," he says in an irritated tone and hands me an orchid with a ripped ribbon. Instead of telling him everything, I stand on the step by the entrance to the building and kiss him so passionately he staggers and accidentally leans back against the rows of buzzers. The gruff voices of all the residents we've woken up come through the speaker. Delighted, we race up to the fourth floor. Inside the apartment I make him some Earl Grey tea and turn on the radio, where a love-struck Peggy Lee's coming down with a fever: *Sun lights up the daytime. Moon lights up the night.* I dim the lights, leaving one sconce on, and I do something I've never done with him around before: I go to the bathroom to take a shower. I return after a quarter of an hour in pajamas, having oiled my body and perfumed it with the remnants of a Dolce Vita sample. As I pass I graze his back with my palm and then stand at the window, behind the curtain. The moon stands out from the darkness and hangs over the city round and glistening like a *Phallus* mushroom.

"Today Saint Jerzy controls the wolves by playing the violin," I whisper to myself, but Kamil hears it.

"Did those sweet little sisters tell you all about the lives of the saints?" he asks. I turn toward him without coming out from behind the curtain.

"It's an old Hutsul legend."

"Oh is it?" He takes two steps forward like in a paso doble. "It's a full moon today, does that mean the wolves will gobble it up?"

I don't respond. The tulle tickles my cheeks. I take two steps forward, like him, and stand in the striated light of the drive. Kamil lifts the curtain slowly like a bride's veil, petting my head, resurrecting once more the sparks in my charged hair, and then he slips his hand under my pajama top and softly caresses my smaller, but more sensitive, left breast. I pull back. Maybe because of what happened at the Dwernicki Market I still need a few moments to absorb. I look down at my hands. Under my fingernails linger patches of white paint like cabbage butterfly wings. Fear pulses under the painful skin on my forearm, flushes my cheeks. The adrenaline heightens my arousal. I stand focused for a moment, my eyes gleaming like a panther readying itself for the attack, but I don't know what to do. In the end he can't take it anymore, he takes me by the hand and leads me to the table. He pulls down my pajama bottoms and sets me on the tabletop. In the darkness I can hear the sound of his belt buckle hit the wood. In the end the fear passes. I wrap my thighs around his waist and use my hand to help him enter me.

And all I am aware of is a rhythm, a rhythm that casts my adolescent body into dark warm depths. His tongue is muscular and gentle. His pubic hair in tiny spirals and soft. The moles on his abdomen like the axis of the Big Dipper. The head of his penis satin and bittersweet to the taste. The way he looks at me, like a wild creature, penetrates me, absorbs me, gets deep inside of me, and in the last spasm becomes me.

An hour later I'm lying naked under the blanket and can remember little of what's just happened. It hurts inside, but not like I'd expected. The first time for those in love, I think, for those who've waited for each other so many months, is like rafting a fast-moving river or leaping right into a waterfall. "I love you," he repeats as he takes me on the mattress, on the floor and against the wall. Afterwards he always holds me and kisses me firmly on the forehead. "There's something in you I can't quite name. That attracts me to you. Some sorts of strange quality, I think. You're sometimes more animal than human. You're like Krajewski's Podolanka being brought up in the cellar, or Rousseau's child of nature, you have an extra sense that on the one hand distances you from people, but on the other brings you closer to them and lets you see inside them. Wouldn't you say?"

He's really laying it on thick, I think, and remember the day he came over for the first time in his Fiat, right after the fields had been blessed, when behind the miniature chapels languished broken elderberry and aspen branches tied with ribbons. It was a Sunday. He got out of his Fiat and slipped on the wet grass. Watching him through the broken window in the attic, I had burst out laughing.

After my grandmother's death, my grandfather broke down. He gave the impression of not really being there anymore, spending whole days just digging or wandering around in the fields. What was strange was that in spite of his mourning he took a liking to Kamil's visits. Every week he'd change into his Sunday best, and pleased as punch someone would want to write down his little folk songs, he'd crack the door to his room with his poker and holler to me, "Kiddo, go and take a look where the road is, see if that city man's a-comin'."

"When you quit coming to see us, I still went out to the road every day to check if your Fiat wasn't up there on the hill," I confess. "Now I think I must have picked Polish literature in Częstochowa just so I'd see you again."

"I wanted to keep coming." He sits down on the mattress and gropes blindly for the lighter tossed onto the floor. "But your mother . . ."

"My mother?" I interrupt him in surprise, and as the one with better night vision I pick up the lighter off the floor. The flint sparks. A little pale blue flame illuminates his face.

"Towards the end of the summer she stopped me by the crossroads and gave me to understand I shouldn't be coming around anymore because, she said, I'm too old and too married for you."

"Married?"

I feel weak, so I lean against the cool wall. I try to breathe, but the air in the room sets and gets rough, scratching in my throat, getting stuck in my gullet. So that was why he was always going away to Katowice: he was going to see his wife, not his mother, I think.

He notices I'm not feeling well and takes me out onto the balcony. We sit facing each other on plastic chairs. Kamil, glancing over at me again and again, smokes down his cigarette, ashing on the drive in front of the building. Flashes cut across the darkness and fall straight onto the concrete.

We go back to the bedroom, where he tells me all about himself now, acquainting me with each of the different stages of his life: his childhood in a big Communist building like this one, college, his older sister who emigrated from Poland, his overworked mother, and finally his father, who was killed in 1981 in the pacification of the Wujek Coal Mine.

Focused on the rhythm of his disjointed tale, I steal a glance at the window. Past the glass something is setting, seeming to enclose us forever inside this stuffy space that is filled with the smells of our bodies. Kamil lies next to me on the mattress, wrapped up in the sheets as though he's just come out of a shroud. A smile lingers on his face. We've been meeting on weekends for weeks now. He brings me gifts: books, lace lingerie, jewelry, perfumes, brand-name clothing I try on and place in a box at the bottom of my wardrobe.

He is ten years older than I am, I think, examining his face with surgical precision, but then again that is exactly what attracted me at first: the crow's feet, the furrows around his nose, the slack skin of his neck and those first gray hairs amidst that otherwise dark brown mop. I'm sure if he were younger, I would never pay him any mind.

Wild thoughts spoil the charm of our night together. I wonder if I could spend my whole life with him. Staring at the wall, where between the slats of the bamboo flower stand a spider web trembles in the draft, to my surprise I start to think about Piotrek. So Kasia wasn't Piotrek's girlfriend, just his cousin? I recall the words of one of the skinheads who attacked me several weeks ago at the Wały Dwernickiego. Sorrow causes my stomach to cramp. I press my face into the pillow and allow my tears to soak into its case.

When I have calmed down, I remember that summer day when my older female cousins from Siemianowice took me to the Fala watering hole in Chorzów.

We spend half the day bathing in the warm water. We never say a word about the fact that nearby, in the park, at dawn, some unknown perpetrator murdered my mom's older sister, Aunt Ania, as she was on her way to work. The newspapers have long since dropped the matter, but I am unable to forget.

One day my mom gets a postcard from Canada signed with her sister's name: "Andzia." She gets pale, stares terrified for a moment at the panorama of Toronto and then tosses the postcard into the furnace. I want to hold her back, I reach my hand out, but the paper is already burning on the hot lumps of coke and curling up into a brown roll. My mom locks herself in the dining room, takes some Diazepam, and sobs on the sofa bed under a cover.

"She was there, she was there in the morgue!" she screams. "I saw her, I identified her body." There is a moment of doubt. "But what if it wasn't her, what if it was just somebody who looked exactly like her? It was summer, it was so hot when those kids playing soccer found her in Silesia Park."

The sun pierces the basins of the pools, alters the smell and color of our young, chlorine-infused bodies, is scattered out across the orange tennis courts, undermines the towers with its heat, finally snags on the pole of the television tower. My cousin and I hold hands and leap into the water gleefully, like nothing even happened a few years ago, like we could trust the world again. An ice stream flows down, but instead of the coolness I expected, probably due to a short-lived thermal shock that deceives my synapses, I feel a painful burn on my skin.

"ARE YOU THERE, GIRL? Are you there?" I hear my grandpa Władek's voice and look around the room. At the open window the curtain puffs up. 'Sleepin' outdoors, sleeping outdoors, a night outside with things to eat and things to eat but not a way to cook 'em,' so we sang in September with the infantry regiment where I was a rifleman in the second company. Now nobody goes and sleeps outdoors. I knew right away it would turn out like this once we quit reaping with the scythe. The boys all came around, started working to drain the land, and then that little creek what went through our fields dried clear up, and the little holy spring did, too. And just look at them taking down the crosses, pretty soon there won't be nowhere to get the fields blessed. Who even goes and gets their fields blessed nowadays? Young people today are stuff and nonsense. When the wheat would break out come May, darlin', remember how that'd look? Hektary would be waves of it. Fields like a sheet would flow in the May breeze, and a person would be lifted up on it, and all the weight would fall clear of his heart. And at the end of the month we'd put the crosses up. Made from lilac branches and alder altars. The womenfolk would bring the vestments and the flowers and the ribbons, but it wasn't ever about those adornments for us, not really. It was something greater. A person would sow the fields, and sleep in the fields, and then he'd bless the fields—now he mows the chapel down instead. That's all gone the way of the dodo now. Devil's cropped up in the quarries, mangled up Hektary. Nightmares is the only dreams. Boboks orbiting around in them. You know I got all the way over to Sarni Stok, over to Świnice, Koziegłówki, and now they told me that ain't Sarni Stok, but Rzeniszanka by the map, but I got a different map in my head, you know, girl? I can find my way anywhere with my eyes closed. Where I'm going now, girl, I don't need a map. And it's time for me to go, I suppose. My bones ache, my soul aches. I just come out a minute, just to have a little talk with you, and see the fields. Over there, in the garden under the window a lupine used to flower, and in that corner there was a pear tree, and over there, in those blackthorn bushes your papa hid from the militia. Uff! And right here I put piles of stone, and there was an orchard, which isn't there no more because a storm took it, but I see it, because when a person really looks, then he sees everything. We're chaff, chaff, understand? In a beam of light that trickles down into a dark barn through an eye in a board.

So go on, girl. May you be blessed with fortune, health, may you be rich in wheat and peas, not only in the summertime, but even in winter may it be sublime.

AS THE BIRDS BEGIN to chatter I awake exhausted, since on my last night in my studio in the development on Lelewel, a few days after separating from Kamil, I was unable to sleep, and then I tossed and turned in my sheets until nine, recalling all those years spent in Częstochowa, day by day, minute by minute, Natka Roszenko, Alex, Sergei, Ludmila, Waldek, whom I still choose to think of as a storyteller and property manager, Mother Stanisława, Sister Zyta, and above all Piotrek and Sister Anna, whom I miss the most.

Did all this really happen? Over the course of three years, from the day I got off at the train station, I have lived like a pupa bound up in its chrysalis; I have carried my suitcase down a road I've let others determine for me, choosing roles for me to play, giving me direction.

I set an envelope with my last month's rent beside the sugar bowl behind the glass of the cupboard, I pick up the phone and ask for the special price to the train station, and then I go out and into the bathroom to wash up and get ready. I look in the mirror. My lips are swollen, my cheeks scraped up by stubble, darkening hickeys on my neck. Kamil has given me back the body I had always chosen to forget before. Even though it's been several months since what happened at the Dwernicki Market, my left forearm is still sore. The moon on the edges of the mirror dictates the last score. The water from the tap drips rhythmically: drip, drip, Caprice in A Minor. Without a doubt Saint Jerzy is playing that melody of Paganini's today. The invisible instruments seize at their strings. The violin music has reached me, but I don't want to listen to it closely, give in to it or even hum its melody.

I press my hands hard against the cold enamel, and then I scream—tentative at first, like a frightened child lost in the woods, crying out for her mother, terrified, but then louder and louder, until finally it's so loud the whole building can hear me, and all three Avenues and Jasna Góra combined.

ACKNOWLEDGMENTS

The citation on page 33 comes from *Urania*, Nr 3 (65), June 1939 , "The Structure of the Milky Way According to Lindblad's Theory," by Dr. W. Iwanowska, of Vilnius.

WIOLETTA GREG is a Polish writer based in the UK. Between 1998–2012 she published six poetry volumes, as well as a novel, *Swallowing Mercury*, which spans her childhood and her experience of growing up in Communist Poland and was longlisted for the Man Booker International Prize. Her works have been translated into seven languages.

JENNIFER CROFT is the recipient of Fulbright, PEN, Tin House, MacDowell, and National Endowment for the Arts grants and fellowships, as well as the inaugural Michael Henry Heim Prize for Translation. Her translation of Olga Tokarczuk's *Flights* won the 2018 Man Booker International Prize.

Transit Books is a nonprofit publisher of international and American literature, based in Oakland, California. Founded in 2015, Transit Books is committed to the discovery and promotion of enduring works that carry readers across borders and communities. Visit us online to learn more about our forthcoming titles, events, and opportunities to support our mission.

TRANSITBOOKS.ORG